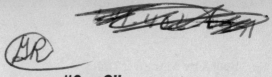

"Cara?"

Connor's deep, husky voice intruded into her thoughts.

"Are you all right?"

She tried to shrug away the emotions drenching her. "I'm fine." She marched over to the safe covered by a portrait of her mother. "I don't understand why he kept this in here. He didn't love her." When she opened the safe, its emptiness surprised her. "This doesn't bode well."

"So someone could have come in here and broken into the safe?"

She turned at the same time Connor stepped closer. She collided into him. He steadied her, his hands on her arms branding her. His gaze captured hers and held it for a long moment, the thundering of her heart drowning out all common sense.

Why else would she wonder if he still kissed as good as he did when they were dating?

Books by Margaret Daley

MARGARET DALEY

feels she has been blessed. She has been married more than thirty years to her husband, Mike, whom she met in college. He is a terrific support and her best friend. They have one son, Shaun. Margaret has been writing for many years and loves to tell a story. When she was a little girl, she would play with her dolls and make up stories about their lives. Now she writes these stories down. She especially enjoys weaving stories about families and how faith in God can sustain a person when things get tough. When she isn't writing, she is fortunate to be a teacher for students with special needs. Margaret has taught for more than twenty years and loves working with her students. She has also been a Special Olympics coach and has participated in many sports with her students.

PROTECTING HER OWN

Margaret Daley

Love Inspired

Recycling programs
for this product may
not exist in your area.

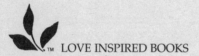 LOVE INSPIRED BOOKS

ISBN-13: 978-0-373-44444-1

PROTECTING HER OWN

www.LoveInspiredBooks.com

Printed in U.S.A.

God is our refuge and strength,
a very present help in trouble.
—*Psalm* 46:1

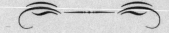

To Jan for all her help and
brainstorming with this story—thank you, Jan.

ONE

"I thought that was taken care of." Cara Madison gripped her cell to her ear so tightly her hand ached as she hurried toward the foyer of her childhood home to answer the door. Exhaustion clung to her as though woven into every fiber of her being.

The bell chimed again.

"No, the State Department still has some questions," Kyra Morgan, her employer at Guardians, Inc., said.

"Hold it a sec. Someone's at the door."

She peered through the peephole, noting a deliveryman with a package and clipboard, dressed in a blue ball cap, blue shorts and white T-shirt. Probably another birthday present from one of Dad's friends. She thrust open the door and cradled the cell against her shoulder to keep it in place.

"So I have to make a trip into Washington, D.C., to see Mr. Richards at the State Department?" Cara asked her boss while she scribbled her name on the sheet of paper then took the box.

Stepping back into the house, Cara shut the door with a nudge of her hip and carried the package to the round table in the center of the dining room to put it with the multitude of others—all presents from people around the world whom her father knew.

"Cara, I'm sorry you need to go at this time. I know that last assignment was rough and now with bringing your dad home from the rehabilitation center, you don't need this complication. Mr. Richards assured me it's just a debriefing about the riots occurring in Nzadi."

She wished she could say that wasn't her fault, but what she did had set the protests off. Guilt swamped her. In protecting her client, a revered humanitarian in Nzadi was killed instead. "Don't worry. I'm tough. I'll survive. I'll call the man and set up an appointment after I get Dad home and settled."

For a few seconds she studied the plain brown box from *Global Magazine* with *C. Madison* on the label before peeling back the top flap on the carton. The sound of the tape ripping the cardboard reverberated in the stillness, exposing the top of a gift wrapped in black paper. Black? True, her father was turning sixty tomorrow, but wasn't black wrapping a little too macabre after he suffered a stroke eight weeks ago?

"I'm sure it's only a formality." Her boss's assurance drew Cara's thoughts away from the gift. "My impression from the State Department was you won't have to go back to answer any more questions from the Nzadi government."

The word *Nzadi* shivered down her length, leaving a track of chills even though it was summer. "I'll call you after I talk to Mr. Richards. Bye." Cara clicked off and stared down at the open box that nestled the new present, wrapped in black paper. Black like people wore to funerals. Black as the dress of the beloved lady who had been killed in the café. Cara shivered again. She wanted to forget Nzadi, but she didn't think she ever would.

The image of the beautiful woman, bleeding out on the floor of the café, nudged those last days in the African country to the foreground. She'd managed to push the trophy wife she was protecting out of the way of the assassin's bullet, only to have it lodge in the woman across from them. Again she heard the angry shouts from the crowd as she'd been driven to the Nzadian airport. The people's grief over the death of Obioma Dia had evolved into fury at Cara and the woman she'd been assigned to protect.

A shrill whistle pierced the air.

Shaking the image and the shouts from her mind, she glanced toward the kitchen. The water she was heating for her tea. The noise insisted on her immediate attention and grated her frazzled nerves. But the sound was a welcome reprieve from the thoughts never far away.

She quickly headed toward the kitchen and a soothing cup of tea along with a moment to rest and think about her father's situation—the reason she was in Clear Branch. She craved peace after the past couple of hectic days—after her last disastrous bodyguard assignment in a country that fell apart around her. Nzadi was still suffering the worst unrest in decades.

Just inside the kitchen she pocketed her phone, wishing she could silence it like she could the teakettle's racket. But her cell was her lifeline, especially when she was on a job. And now also because her dad's homecoming celebration was cancelled because of a reaction to a new medication that made the doctor decide at the last minute to keep him a few more days. She'd planned a small birthday party for tomorrow and would need to finish calling his friends to tell them she'd have to postpone the festivity.

As steam shot out of the spout on the white pot, she snatched it off the burner and set it on a cool spot on the stove. Finally the loud, annoying sound quieted. She turned toward the cabinet behind her to get a mug.

Blissful silence—no angry people in Nzadi yelling words that still curdled her blood, no rehabilitation center—

A boom rocked the foundation beneath her feet. She flew back and slammed against the edge of the counter so hard the air rushed from her lungs. Her momentum then spun her to the side, her hip clipping the corner. Her head swung back against the freezer handle then forward. Darkness swirled before her eyes as bits of wood and plaster rained down upon her, stinging her skin. Her ears rang, drowning out any sound except the thundering of her heartbeat vying for dominance.

She fumbled at her waist for the gun she wore on the job. Nothing. An urgency hammered her. Then scanning her surroundings, she realized it was on her nightstand in her bedroom. She looked toward what used to be the door from the dining room, trying to clear the haze in her mind. To figure out what to do.

Assess the situation.

Part of the wall was gone and gray smoke bellowed through the opening, carrying dust, wood chips and black bits. The wrapping paper? The stench of black powder assaulted her nostrils. She coughed, squinting to see through the ominous cloud invading every corner of the kitchen. She swiped at her gritty eyes but stopped in midaction, afraid to rub them anymore for fear of damaging them.

Need some kind of weapon.

She started toward the drawer a few feet away from her. Her legs gave out. Crumpling down the refrigerator to the tile floor, she grabbed at the dish towel hanging over the edge of the counter nearby and covered her mouth and nose with it. The room continued to rotate as though gravity were playing some kind of cruel joke on her. With a gong clanging against her skull from the concussion of the blast, she rolled over onto her knees and pushed up. The room swayed and she fell back.

She groped for her cell in her pocket and managed to slip it out, but her hand trembled so much she dropped it on the debris-covered tile.

Got to pull myself together. I've been in tough situations before.

To still the thundering of her heartbeat, she took a moment and inhaled steadying breaths through the filtering material of the towel. More coughs racked her.

Stay calm. Call 911.

She flipped the phone open while it still rested on the floor and began punching in the numbers. Drawing in another deep breath, she lifted it to her ear. The shrill ringing in her ears persisted. She doubted she could hear the 911 operator, but she needed help even getting up.

She waited a few seconds, hoping the 911 operator had answered, then said into the cell, "I can't hear you. I need help. Cara—Madison." Panic began to worm its way into her mind. With her hand holding the phone quivering, she quickly finished, "Explosion. 218 North Pine. Hurry."

Did I get through?

The cell slipped from her nerveless fingers. Still connected to 911, she hoped, she left the phone next to her while she clutched the dish towel against her face. All she wanted to do now was collapse to the cold, dirty tiles and close her eyes to still the spinning. And wait to be rescued. Dust and debris from the dining room coated the floor, a reminder of what just happened. A thought nagged her.

As a bodyguard for the past four years, she'd had one assignment where an explosion had been involved. She tried to remember back to that job her first year, but her thoughts swirled like the gray smoke earlier. What if the blast wasn't the only one? What if it ignited a fire?

Trained to remain calm in chaotic situations, she shoved her rising panic down and crawled toward the back door. A stab of pain emanated from her hip that had hit the counter, making her progress laborious. The dizziness from her movement threatened to swallow her. She had to slow down her pace even more. The scent of sulfur hung in the hazy, smoked-filled kitchen. Another spasm of coughing assailed her. Every muscle tensed as the minutes ticked by, and yet she was still only halfway to her escape. A chunk of Sheetrock crashed to the floor near her, dust mushrooming into the air. Glancing up, she spied cracks in the ceiling. Her heart jammed into her throat.

"Well, as I live and breathe, Connor Fitzgerald here in my station." Sheriff Taylor pumped Connor's arm as he shook his hand. "What brings you down here?"

"Can't an old friend visit?" Connor grinned at the taller man, several years older than his own age of thirty-four.

"Come in and tell me how it's going." Sean Taylor waved his hand toward one of two chairs in front of his desk. "How's it going at Virginia's Criminal Intelligence Division?"

"Work's good. Busy." Connor folded his long length into the chair, resting his elbows on the padded arms. "I'm here for a week to spend some time with Gramps rather than my usual one or two days. He gets lonely. He claims all his contemporaries are dying off."

"Your grandfather continues to surprise me. He's eighty and still going strong."

"Yup, that's him."

"At least you aren't too far away in Richmond."

The door opened and a deputy stuck his head into the

room. "Sheriff, there's been a 911 call from Cara Madison at her dad's. She reported an explosion at the house. I dispatched two deputies and called Doc Sims."

Cara's here? She's hurt? Connor sat up straight, his gut tightening. "Who's injured?"

"Don't know. All she said was there was an explosion and that she couldn't hear well. The 911 operator tried to get more information from her but couldn't."

Sean snatched up his keys. "Thanks." Turning toward Connor, he continued, "Want to come? I know you and Cara go way back."

Connor nodded and rose. He hadn't seen her in years, and the last time they hadn't parted on good terms. He'd wanted her to stay in Clear Branch and marry him. She'd wanted to see the world. She'd left the next day.

"I'll follow you in my car," Connor said as he strode with Sean toward the exit.

Cara's father knew a lot of important people in Virginia as well as Washington, D.C. If someone was after him, the Criminal Investigative Department of the Virginia State Police could be called in to assist with the case. Since Connor was an investigator for the CID, he might as well check on what happened. That was the only reason he was going. *Yeah, right, as if you don't want to make sure Cara's okay.*

In his Jeep Cherokee, Connor pulled out of the parking lot right behind the sheriff's vehicle. Although his gaze focused on the white car with the flashing lights and siren in front of him, his thought centered on Cara, the only woman who had captured his heart and then crushed it. If Virginia's CID *was* called in, that didn't mean the case had to be his problem. He could probably claim conflict of interest. He didn't need another problem on his plate.

Cara hadn't been his concern for thirteen years. So why was he going to the Madison house?

He couldn't shake the question: Was she all right? The last he'd heard anything about her she'd quit her job as an investigative reporter for a major TV network. But that was five years ago. Didn't Gramps say something about her becoming a bodyguard? Whenever his grandfather tried to talk about Cara, Connor had always changed the subject. Now he wished he'd listened for once.

Then another question popped into his thoughts as he turned onto Pine Street in Clear Branch: *Why do I care?*

A fire truck and two deputies' cars were parked in front of a sprawling ranch-style home with a gaping hole where a large picture window in the dining room used to be. Bits of that window and brick around it littered the yard. He'd wanted his detached, professional facade to slip into place, but the sight of the damage the explosion had caused shoved his concern to the foreground. Fear spurred his heartbeat.

Lord, in spite of our history, I don't want Cara hurt.

Climbing from his Jeep, he surveyed the quiet, well-to-do neighborhood. Several people stood on their lawns observing the commotion. His long strides ate up the distance between him and Sean, who had finished talking to a firefighter and was heading toward the gaping hole in the house.

Check to make sure she's in one piece. Then leave.

"A gas explosion?" Connor asked, taking a whiff of the air. Nothing hinted at that, but he did smell a faint odor of sulfur as though someone had recently shot off some fireworks. Alarm bells went off in his mind. "Since C.J. had his stroke, is he still working for Global News?"

"You smell it, too, don'tcha?"

"Yup, black powder."

"He's still at Sunny Meadows, but if I know C.J., he'll be back to his old desk as soon as humanly possible. He was supposed to be home today."

"Where's Cara?" What if she'd passed out somewhere in the house after she made the 911 call? What if there was another bomb? He quickened his steps toward the front door, which was barely hanging on its hinges.

A hand on his arm halted his progress. "I've called the tri-county task force's bomb squad. Also, ATF. I don't want anyone inside until they clear it. Even the firefighters will stay back unless a fire breaks out."

"But Cara?" *Lord, she has to be okay.*

Sean tossed his head in the direction of the side of the house. "My deputy has her. He found her out back. She's okay."

Connor turned and saw one of the deputies and Cara making their way slowly across the lawn. For a few seconds his heartbeat pummeled against his rib cage at the disheveled sight of her—alive but hurt. He forced his emotions concerning her into a box and slammed the lid closed, searching for that professional facade so necessary for him to do his job.

The officer had his arm around Cara and supported most of her weight. The sight of tiny cuts scoring her face constricted Connor's chest. He forced a stabilizing breath into his lungs, but the band around him contracted even more as the sounds of her coughing competed with the murmurs from the neighbors gathering. Her blue eyes were huge as though she'd been caught at a surprise birthday party. Her short russet hair, which had always been long when he'd known her before, was dusty gray to match the rest of her.

His gaze zeroed in on her full lips, the corners turned down at the moment. He could remember that when she'd smile at him, it would take over her whole expression. The knot in his gut hardened at the pain reflected in her expression.

As he neared her, he noticed the trembling in her arms dangling at her sides, the slight limp as she favored her right leg. Her owlish gaze locked with his, and for a few seconds no recognition dawned in them. Had he changed that much? He hadn't thought so.

Then a light flickered in the blue depths. Her mouth curved up briefly. "Connor, you're home," she said in a raspy voice.

He had thought his stomach couldn't tighten any more than it had. But it did. Into a ball of steel, burning its way clear up to his heart.

No way! I won't go to that place ever again. The vow tempered the fiery need to hold her and run his arms over her to make sure she wasn't seriously injured.

He cocked a grin, stopping a foot from her and the deputy. "What kind of trouble have you gotten yourself into this time?"

She swallowed hard, tried to smile again and failed. She squinted and focused on his lips, then shook her head and pointed to her ears. "Can't hear you." A thread of panic edged her words.

The sheriff wrote on his pad that he'd sent a deputy to Sunny Meadows to stay with her dad and held it up for Cara.

"Thanks." Relief flittered over her face, only to be replaced by the pain again.

Sean jotted something on his pad then showed Cara.

"Not a gas explosion. House is all electric." That word ended on a cough.

Out of the corner of his eye, Connor saw a car pull up

to the curb behind the fire truck and Doc Sims climb from the vehicle.

The short, portly man leaned in, withdrew a black bag, then hurried around to the other side and opened the back door. "Let's get her over here so I can check her out."

"I'm sure you have something to do. I can take her from here," Connor said to the deputy, a part of himself amazed that he'd volunteered to hold Cara, have her flush up against him.

His arm coiled about her. The fragrance of lilacs, mingling with the odors of sulfur and dust, wafted to him. The flowery scent teased his memories of days gone by and vied with another—the apple-scented shampoo she'd always used. Some things hadn't changed. These smells brought up memories of the past when he'd loved her.

But she'd killed that feeling the day she'd left town without even saying goodbye. She'd disappeared from his life only to reappear several years later reporting the news from a Southeast Asian country in the midst of a rebellion. Chaos had ruled the scene behind her. And yet she'd been calm, totally charged with the action occurring around her. So much like her father when he'd been reporting about a volatile situation.

That had been his Cara. A thrill seeker. Restless. Needing something she couldn't find in Clear Branch.

But it felt right with her in his arms again.

His thoughts prodded his steps faster until she halted, making him stop, too. She blinked as though trying to orient herself to her surroundings.

"Slow down," she said in a voice that had been heard around the world for years until she suddenly dropped out of sight five years ago. "Dizzy."

He'd let her get to him. Angry with himself, he clenched his jaws and nodded. At a much slower pace he covered the distance to Doc Sims and eased Cara onto the backseat. The doctor whipped out a blanket and draped it over Cara's shoulders, sending up a cloud of dust that aggravated her coughing. Connor stepped away as the doctor began examining her.

"Do you hurt anywhere?" Doc Sims asked.

Her face crunched up into a frown and she started to say something when Connor replied, "She can't hear. The blast."

"I was hoping she hadn't been that close to the explosion." Doc looked from her to Connor. "I'll take it from here." A smile accompanied the dismissal.

Connor backpedaled for a few paces then swung around and went in search of the sheriff. Nothing would be discovered until the bomb squad arrived, but he was itching to do a walk-through. This wasn't his area of expertise, though, and he would have to wait.

Was the bomb meant for Cara or her dad? Most likely her dad. But if Cara was still working as a bodyguard, it was possible she had angered someone.

The sheriff rounded the corner from the side and strode to Connor. "I got a call that the bomb squad should be here shortly. I didn't find anything suspicious in the backyard. I looked in the kitchen window and saw part of the ceiling on the floor. Cara's lucky she got out okay. Is Doc going to call for the ambulance in Silver Creek or take her to his clinic?"

Since Clear Branch was small with a population of four thousand, the ambulance would have to come from the larger town twenty minutes away. "I don't know. He dismissed me."

"That's our doc."

"Do you think the bomb was meant for C.J.?"

"For over thirty years he was in the middle of any

important newsworthy situation in the world working for Global News Organization. His exposé on the Mafia alone would have ruffled people's feathers. Not to mention he'd decided to write his memoir. Planned on naming names and exposing corruption in high places. People that may have escaped prosecution but not the power of the pen— his words, not mine. So, yeah, I think someone could have a grudge against him."

"Maybe the memoir is the key, and that sparked this attack now."

Sean rubbed his hand through his hair. "Maybe, but he hadn't started it yet. Cara has done her fair share of things that would make enemies."

"As a bodyguard?"

"She's worked a couple of high-profile assignments."

"So you think she could be in danger?"

"Maybe. But if I had to pick one I would pick C.J. He's got the manners of a pit bull and a rattlesnake all rolled up in one, especially when he's on a hot story."

As much as he wished he didn't, he still held feelings for Cara. Connor's own relief, though, that C.J. was probably the target rather than Cara eased the tautness from his muscles. There was no love lost between her dad and him. "Where's she living now?" Why was he asking? Stay away.

"Dallas, when she isn't traveling for Guardians, Inc."

He'd heard of the group of all female bodyguards. Its reputation was top-notch. Connor looked toward where Doc was still checking Cara out. *Lord, I wasn't prepared to see her again.* "Do you think she'll go back to Dallas soon?"

"I don't know if she's going back just yet. She's trying to get something set up so her father can live at home and receive the therapy he needs for his recovery. He's been getting better. I was surprised this morning when she called to tell me the birthday party she'd planned for tomorrow at the house was canceled because her dad would be at Sunny Meadows a few more days."

"She doesn't have anywhere to stay now," Connor murmured, looking at the bombed-out front of the house. If he'd realized Cara was back in town, he wouldn't have come home. Gramps had failed to mention that when he'd talked to him last night before coming from Richmond.

"There's always the hotel on Main Street since the lodge by the lake is full with Labor Day approaching. But I'm figuring she needs someone to watch over her until we can piece together what's going on. Who the target is."

Connor chuckled. "I don't envy you that job."

"I don't have the manpower to watch over her adequately and C.J. at the center as well as try to solve this case. But you could protect Cara."

"Oh, no." Connor shook his head, stepping away from his friend to emphasize he didn't want anything to do with Cara Madison. "I'd rather be in a pit full of rattlesnakes," he said in all seriousness, thinking about the sheriff's reference to a rattlesnake earlier.

Sean burst out laughing. "I hear where she lives they have rattlesnake roundups. Maybe you could visit her and go to one." A serious expression descended. "I need someone I trust. Your grandfather lives on the outskirts of town on a few acres. Quiet. Between you and your grandfather, she ought to be safe just in case we're wrong and she's the target."

"And just how do you think I can keep her at Gramps's house?"

"I know that will be impossible, but when she comes into town, you can be with her. Your place is defensible, better than a hotel. Your grandfather has an alarm system.

The terrain around his place is open, and the area is a quiet neighborhood without a lot of people."

"You make it sound like I should be planning for a war."

"Well, not exactly. Just pointing out why your grand-father's house is perfect, and I'll sleep a whole lot better knowing she's being taken care of."

"And I should care why?" The tension in Connor's neck spread down his spine and radiated across his shoulders.

"Because when I get a good night's sleep, I can actu-ally function pretty good and might just be able to find out who's trying to kill one of the Madisons."

But I won't get a bit of sleep, Connor wanted to shout at his friend.

"It shouldn't be more than a week at most, and you know your grandfather has a soft spot for Cara. I wouldn't be surprised if when he hears about the situation, he won't insist she come stay with you guys. And her dad, too, when he's discharged from Sunny Meadows."

The thought of being in the same house as C.J. increased the pain gripping his shoulders. Connor leaned toward Sean and lowered his voice. "I won't tell Gramps."

"But every busybody in this town will. So cut your losses and just agree now. He probably already knows."

There was a part of him that really meant what he'd said about her not staying with him and Gramps, but there was a part that knew if he looked deep down, every one of those words was a lie. As angry as he was at Cara, he never wanted anything bad to happen to her or her father, and there was no way he could walk away without helping to keep her safe.

His gaze strayed to Cara, still pale with a fine layer of dust covering her, her hand not quite steady as she held out her palm for a pill from Doc Sims. A wet streak down her face stirred feelings in Connor he'd kept locked away for thirteen years. Cara never cried. Living with her iron-willed father had made her tough. The sight pricked his conscious. He couldn't turn his back on her, and all the protests in the world weren't going to change that.

"Okay, I know when to admit I'm defeated. She can stay at Gramps's." He swallowed the lump lodged in his throat and muttered through clenched teeth, "And so can C.J."

Sean slapped him on the back. "That's great. Then we're set."

"Are we? You've forgotten one important piece in all of this." At his friend's raised eyebrow, Connor continued, "You have to get Cara to agree to stay there."

TWO

The softness beneath her cheek tempted Cara to surrender again to the dark void of sleep. She shifted, aches protesting the move. Slowly she raised one eyelid and stared at an unfamiliar chest of drawers.

Where am I?

The last thing she remembered was Connor coming into the clinic to check on her. At least that was what she thought. Or was it a dream? When she tried to think about the morning, everything blurred, as though she were looking through sheers into a room and not quite seeing it clearly.

Her head throbbing where she'd struck the refrigerator, she cautiously rolled over, opening both eyes to stare at a white ceiling. She searched the dimly lit room. The beige blinds were closed. Little gave away where she was. *A hotel room? Still at Doc Sims's clinic?*

She eased up on her elbows to get a better look, conscious of not moving too fast. The room didn't spin. Her world was stable. Then she zoomed in on a sound coming from her left. A rhythmic ticking. She glanced at the nightstand, which had only a lamp and a clock on it.

7:00? She glanced toward the window, muted light leaking through the slats in the blinds.

What happened to the past eight hours? Is Dad all right?

She jerked up straight in bed and immediately regretted that sudden movement. After the dizziness passed, she swung her legs to the floor and rose slowly, glad she was still dressed in her dust-covered jeans and a University of Virginia T-shirt that Doc had at his clinic. The room held nothing personal in it, only the bed, two nightstands on either side of it, a chest of drawers and a comfortable-looking maroon chair near the one window with a little round table next to it.

The room is void of any feeling—like my life of late.

Cara pushed that thought away. She had more important concerns than piecing her life back together. She needed to discover who wanted her dad dead. And that meant getting answers from the sheriff.

But first, is Dad okay at Sunny Meadows? She looked around for a phone since she'd left her cell back on her father's kitchen floor. No phone.

Needing to find out where she was and call the rehabilitation center, she limped toward the door, the pain in her hip and head a nagging reminder of what had happened earlier. Out in a hallway of what appeared to be a house, vague memories of the past tugged at her. Seeing a bathroom door open, she slipped inside and washed off what grime was left on her face and neck then finger-combed her hair into a semblance of order. Cuts on her skin emphasized the ordeal she'd gone through.

She heard voices coming from her right. Heading that way, she soon entered a kitchen she had known all too well as a young woman and came to a halt when her gaze fell upon Connor Fitzgerald. So she hadn't dreamed him. He had been at her dad's house earlier, and she was at his grandfather's now.

Connor fastened his hard, slate-gray eyes on her. The chill from that look went straight to her bones.

"I was getting worried about you, child."

Cara shifted her attention to the wiry, old man with bright alert eyes. Mike Fitzgerald sat opposite his grandson. A warm welcome spread across his features as his assessing survey took her in. He rose, still thin with a fit body for his age and a full head of stark white hair. He moved a little slower than she remembered, but with the assurance she'd known, and enveloped her in a bear hug. She winced at the welcoming embrace.

"I'm so glad you're okay and staying here. Me and Connor can keep you safe."

Staying at Connor's grandfather's house? Did she forget something from the morning? All she could remember was lying on Doc's examination table after he took some X-rays. Totally exhausted and hurting, she'd taken something to help her rest. Then Connor had come in and talked with Doc. When she'd closed her eyes, weariness pulling her down toward the dark, another voice, deep and gruff, joined the two men's. Mike's? He'd asked her something and she'd answered. Then she'd drifted off to sleep to the sound of their murmured voices, too tired to care.

What had been Mike's question and my answer?

The scent of coffee floated on the air. She needed caffeine and her brain functioning at one hundred percent before she tackled the man across from Mike Fitzgerald.

"May I have some coffee? Actually, a whole pot full?"

"Sure, child. Anything I have is yours. You know that." Mike wrapped his calloused hand around hers and guided her toward the table and a seat next to his grandson.

Connor's coldness continued to flow from him and drape her in a blanket of ice. Mike set a big mug of black coffee, the way she took hers, in front of her. She cradled it between her hands to heat her fingers while she waited for it to cool down enough to drink.

"Well, I'll leave you two younguns alone. I imagine you have some catching up to do." Mike hurried toward the hallway as though he knew he needed to escape or risk getting caught in the cross fire.

She itched to drag Connor's grandfather back into the chair on the other side of her, but he could move surprisingly fast when he wanted. Taking a sip of her coffee, she stabbed Connor with what she hoped was a piercing look. "Why am I here?"

"You heard Gramps. Until the person who sent the bomb is caught, you're in danger. The sheriff asked me to watch out for you. Gramps and I brought you here after Doc gave his okay, so long as we kept an eye on you and let him know if there's a problem."

"His okay! How about mine?" Her voice rose as her temper did. "Maybe I'd rather stay somewhere else. Did you think to ask?"

"My grandfather *did*. You can't stay at your dad's house. The damage is extensive in the dining room, foyer and kitchen where part of the doorway and wall blew out."

"You've been inside and seen it?"

He nodded and delved into his pocket, then presented her cell phone to her. "After the bomb squad okayed the premises, I accompanied the sheriff and ATF agents. I found that on the floor and saw it was yours."

"What did they find?" She chanced a sip of the still hot coffee because she needed something to drive the fuzz from her brain. To deal with Connor she *had* to be clearheaded.

"It looks like a pipe bomb, and from the damages a large one. The ATF guys gathered evidence to analyze and will get back to Sean when they have anything to report."

A large pipe bomb. Low-tech but it definitely could have killed her or her dad if they had been closer to it. *Interesting,* the logical, investigative part of her mind reasoned while the other wanted to shut down.

"Cara, who is trying to kill your dad—or you?"

"Me?" She didn't want Connor involved in her life and certainly not protecting her. His nearness brought to the foreground everything she had run away from thirteen years ago. He'd wanted to smother her, do everything for her then. And in the short time they had been reunited, he was doing it again.

"Sean told me what you've been doing these past few years. We can't totally rule you out as a possible target. I mean to find out what's going on."

She locked gazes with Connor and automatically her adrenaline spiked at the challenge—could she put their past aside to let him do his job—that she glimpsed in his depths. "Why? Because of our past?"

Connor rose and crossed to the stove to refill his mug. "Sean has asked for my help and I'm giving it. The origin of the bomb was in the dining room—the table. Do you know what the pipe bomb might have been in?"

Although she'd been forced to leave Nzadi under less than ideal conditions, she didn't think anyone would have followed her to the United States to try and kill her—she hoped. "I don't think I'm the target. My dad had been receiving birthday gifts from friends. The neighbor who had been collecting the mail brought them over yesterday morning. I had a stack of them on the dining room table from people around the world. He'll be sixty tomorrow." If she hadn't been so preoccupied with the Nzadi affair on the phone with Kyra, she might have been more suspicious about the black-wrapped gift. Although black wrapping paper was often used as a joke for a milestone birthday, anyone knowing her father wouldn't have sent a gift wrapped in black paper. He wouldn't be amused.

"Nothing seemed suspicious to you? Your dad wasn't even home—hadn't been for eight weeks."

"But he had been due home this morning right before the last package, a medium-size box wrapped in black paper, was delivered."

"Who knew about that?"

She shrugged, wishing she felt nonchalant. "Everyone in town."

"But he didn't come home."

"It was a last-minute decision by his doctor at Sunny Meadows. He had a reaction to some new medication, and the doctor wanted him to stay there another day or so to keep an eye on him. I'd only been able to tell a few people I needed to cancel his birthday party. Sean was one of them." She narrowed her eyes on him as he sat. "I feel like I'm being interrogated."

"I do work for the Virginia CID." He lifted his mug to his lips and took a long sip.

For a few seconds she watched that action, remembering a time when those lips had kissed hers. She looked down at her drink and tried to bring some kind of order to her chaotic thoughts. "You have no right to bring me here without my permission. I'm sure I didn't give it." She wouldn't have because that meant she would be near Connor. There was no way she could deal with him on top of everything else. "The last thing I recall is lying on Doc's examination table. He gave me another pill and that's all. Did he drug me?"

"He gave you pain medication. You went to sleep all on your own."

Which really didn't surprise her. She had been functioning on only a few hours of sleep for the past four days, reporting to Kyra about her last assignment after escaping Nzadi then turning right around and coming to Clear Branch at midnight two days ago. Although she'd been to the rehabilitation center/nursing home to make plans to move her father to his house, she'd thought she could rest before having to deal with his situation.

But ever since she stepped through the doorway into her childhood home, memories had bombarded her from all sides. She'd spent most of the past two nights prowling the house, trying not to dredge up memories from the last time she'd been there and the fight she and her dad had had. That memory had kept her away for thirteen years.

"And I've been here for how long?"

"Since before noon. As I said, Gramps *did* ask you about coming here."

"And I answered?" Memories of earlier began to leak back into her mind. She remembered the deep, gruff voice saying something to her. Then, because her ears were still ringing, Mike had written something on a piece of paper. The blast must have affected her more than she thought if she'd agreed to come here.

"Yes. Gramps and I brought you here."

"How?"

"I carried you to the car and then to the house."

That was what she'd been afraid of. Her heartbeat sped at the thought of being in Connor's arms, cradled against him—twice in one day. Another memory of being in his arms cloaked her. Of him kissing her. A lifetime ago. "I don't need to be protected. I didn't thirteen years ago, and I don't now. I'm not the one in danger." At least she didn't think so, and she would do her own checking into that. "My dad must be. I need to call the center to see how he is."

She flipped open her cell and punched in the stored

number of Sunny Meadows, then asked to speak to the
nurse on duty. When she came on the line, Cara asked,
"How's C. J. Madison doing? This is his daughter."

"Cara, this is Kathy. Your dad is fine, but the doctor
wants to keep him at least through tomorrow."

"Is the deputy sheriff with him?" she asked, vaguely
recalling Sean writing something to that effect on a piece
of paper.

"Yes. In fact, after the sheriff came a while ago and told
your father what happened, he got quite upset at the news.
It took us a while to get him settled down. Doc had us give
him his sleeping pill early tonight. I think he's down for the
night. Are you all right? Everyone heard what happened at
the house."

Cara had known Kathy in high school and was glad she
was one of the nurses looking after her father. "I'm fine.
So you don't think I should come see him tonight?"

"No. Get a good night's sleep and come tomorrow morning."

Cara snagged Connor's gaze while she said goodbye
to Kathy. "I may have agreed to come here because Mike
asked, but I'm not staying here, Connor."

He surged to his feet and strode to the sink to pitch the
rest of his coffee. "I tried to tell Gramps and the sheriff you
wouldn't want this, but they were sure you would see the
wisdom in being here in an environment a little bit easier
to control than a hotel. They just don't remember how pig-
headed you are."

"Well, then I'll have to tell them after you take me to
the house."

"No can do."

"What do you mean? I need some clean clothes. You
can't keep me here against my will. I'm not in any danger.
Besides, I know how to take care of myself." Her training

and survival instinct had gotten her out of the kitchen before more of the ceiling had come down on top of her.

His smile tilted up the corners of his mouth, but that was all it did, as though he was trying valiantly to be patient. "It'll be dark before we can get to your house, and there's no electricity. It's not safe at night."

Again he was making decisions for her. "Haven't you heard of flashlights?" Standing, she gripped the edge of the table with both hands then leaned into it.

"Haven't you heard of patience? Oh, I forgot that was never one of your strong suits. You always wanted things right then and there."

"Because I left Clear Branch? I didn't want to stay here and settle down. There were things I wanted to do before I married." If she ever married. After seeing her parents' marriage, she wasn't sure that was something she should do. That opinion hadn't changed in thirteen years.

For a few seconds something flickered in and out of his gaze. Hurt? It was gone so fast and quickly replaced by anger that Cara couldn't tell.

Connor's jaw set in a hard line. "You can rummage around in the house tomorrow at first light if you want. I'll even take you now that I'm working the case. The crime scene guys have processed the scene."

Dread rose in her. "Why do you want to work the case? Aren't you here for a visit like I am?"

"Yes, but I'm going to because Sean asked me to help and I've already cleared it with headquarters. So sit and get comfy." He waved his hand toward the chair behind her. "I have some questions for you. Then if you want, I'll take you to the hotel. The house isn't an option for tonight. Personally, I didn't want you here, but Gramps and Sean just might have a point. We don't really know what's going on. Who the target is."

His words hurt, and she tried not to feel that. She didn't love him anymore. She was a totally different person from that twenty-one-year-old who'd left Clear Branch to travel, try her hand at reporting like her father. She'd seen the world, and it had chewed her up and spit her out. Few people knew what had really happened in Nzadi near the Congo River in Africa—only what was splashed all over the news for a day and minus her name connected to it—but she did and she had to live with it.

"I'll try not to trouble you for too long." Cara sank onto the seat, exhaustion deluging her. She needed at least another twenty-four hours of sleep.

He remained at the sink, lounging back against the counter. "So as I asked before, in case you're the target, who would want to kill you?"

"I've irritated a few people through the years." Riding to the airport after the attempt on client's life had been the longest thirty minutes of Cara's life. All the crowd gathered at the airport had known was that the woman who should have died was alive in the limousine and Obioma Dia, who they revered, was dead in her place.

"I'm not surprised." He chuckled.

The sound, a familiar one from her past, eased the tension that left a trail of knotted muscles along her shoulders and neck. "Where should I begin?"

"Just how many do you think there are?"

"We could start with the president of Nzadi. Although he would deny it, he was the one who had me kicked out of his country." Along with the businessman and his wife.

"Yeah, I've read about the riots in Nzadi. All Americans were asked to leave. Let's start closer to home. Who have you ticked off in the U.S.?"

"Besides you?"

An eyebrow arched. "Yeah."

"I've been responsible for putting some people behind bars. I may not be a law enforcement officer like you, but I'm good at my job. I've prevented several people from being hurt and apprehended the person behind the threat. Someone could be upset with me over that." She tilted her chin up a notch. "If you want my cooperation, it will be a joint investigation."

Ignoring her statement, he scowled and said, "I'll need a list of those people you helped put behind bars." His hands flat on the table, he leaned across it. "Why are you visiting now? I know there isn't any love lost between you and your dad unless things have changed since I last saw you."

They hadn't, and in fact they had gotten worse between her and her father, ever since she quit being an investigative reporter. But the unfounded accusation in Connor's voice caused her to straighten her shoulders and stiffen her spine. "There might not be any love lost between my father and me, but I will protect my own. Contrary to what you think, I'm not heartless." The trouble was her heart was filled with too many emotions, laid shattered by all that she'd seen around the world while doing her job, first as an investigative reporter, and then as a bodyguard. The incident in Nzadi sent her home to the States to piece together what little was left of her life. She couldn't keep running away from what was really eating at her: the failure to stop her mother from killing herself when Cara was nineteen years old.

He sighed. His vehement expression evened out into a neutral one. "I never said that, Cara. I know too well what you and your dad were going through right before you left. Remember I had wanted to help."

"Your help only riled Dad more. I told you then I fight my own battles. I don't need a protector."

"It's okay to accept help, and whether you want it now or not, I'll be helping you. This is my case, my problem."

"I know. So where do *we* start?"

"We! There is no *we* in this. You're the victim, not the investigator."

"But—"

"You aren't going to let this go, are you?"

She shook her head. "I can't."

His gaze zoomed in on her. "Are you hiding anything from me?"

"I promise you, no. I've told you all I know. I'll get you that list of people." *But I won't tell you about the woman in Nzadi.* That had been the last straw for her. It was too painful to talk about, especially with Connor. She would not bear her heart to him. Nor with all that had happened between them in the past. "I won't sit quietly by and not do anything. You know me. Won't it be better if I help you, rather than go off on my own? That way you can 'protect me.'"

A laugh escaped his lips, a half grin curling one corner of his mouth. "I was going to leave you here under Gramps's watchful eye."

"Since I'm not staying here, that won't work. Besides, how are you going to protect me if you're out investigating?"

He raked his fingers through his short, dark brown hair. "You are good with twisting things around to suit you."

"That's part of my charm."

"That's a matter of opinion. I should just hand the case over to someone else."

"You won't. I know you. Besides, I don't want you to."

Both eyebrows rose, wrinkling his forehead in puzzlement. "You want me to work on this?"

"I trust you'll do a good job."

"You don't know anything about me now."

"I know the man you were, and I doubt seriously that core of integrity and dedication to whatever you set your mind to has changed. Are you telling me it has?" She pushed to her feet, no longer wanting him to have a height advantage—or rather less of one since he was half a foot taller than her five-nine.

"No, that hasn't, but I'm not that same man. I'm no longer naive and love struck. You pretty well cured that thirteen years ago."

"If this is gonna work, we have to agree to let the past go. I'm not the same. You aren't, either." She stuck her hand out. "Truce? Can we put it behind us at least for the time we're together? Start fresh as though we're strangers?"

He stared at her outstretched arm, then slowly closed his hand around hers and shook it. "Deal. We don't need to fight each other *and* the person who sent that little present today."

"Can you at least take me to pick up my car at the house? I want to drive it to the hotel on Main Street. I'll get a room there. I won't try to go inside the house until tomorrow, but I do need a change of clothing and I have a spare bag in the trunk. I was going to go work out after seeing Dad today."

"Okay."

Twenty minutes later Connor pulled up in front of her childhood home. The almost full moon highlighted the large dark cavity with a heavy plastic sheet over it where the picture window in the dining room had been. She caught glimpses of the boards nailed over the opening. The realization of what had happened that morning slammed into her again. She'd thought coming back to Virginia would give her the sense of stability and normalcy she needed in her life while she tried to figure out what she wanted to do—continue working as a bodyguard or try something else. It hadn't, and when she returned to Dallas she'd need to deal with that.

But right now she just wanted to stay alive and keep her father alive.

"Thanks for the ride. What time should I meet you back here tomorrow morning?"

"I'll come by the hotel and pick you up at eight."

"But I have my own car."

"Together. Remember, Cara?"

"Fine. I'll be in the lobby at eight."

She hurried to her car. Behind her Connor followed. At the driver's door she whirled to face him. "You don't have to—"

"Before you get in, I want to check to make sure there isn't another bomb attached to the car."

THREE

The next morning, Cara paced in front of the Clear Branch Hotel on Main, waiting for Connor to pick her up. She glanced at her watch. 7:55. She'd come down early because she hadn't slept. Her body had protested every position she'd lain in. Finally she decided staying in the room one more minute would cause her to run down the hall stark raving mad.

Another sleepless night. Images of a killer stalking her father flitted in and out of her mind the whole time she lay in bed and stared at the light from the hotel's sign dancing across the ceiling as it swung in the breeze. Although her relationship with her father had been rocky, she didn't want anything to happen to him. She still hoped to feel accepted by him one day. No matter how much she tried not to care, she did.

Her car had checked out. No more bombs had been planted there. Although she didn't think she was the target, as a onetime investigative reporter she knew that she couldn't totally dismiss the idea that she was the one the bomb was meant for. What if something she'd done had brought danger to her father? She had enough self-inflicted guilt, no need to add more on top of it.

Her instinct, which had served her well in the past, told

her that her father was the target. In his line of work, he'd made some powerful enemies. But knowing all that didn't mean she would let down her guard, especially since she felt this wouldn't be the only attempt if they didn't discover who was behind the bombing.

What was she going to do when the doctor released her dad from Sunny Meadows? After escorting her to her hotel room the night before, Connor had left her with that question and an invitation for both of them to stay with him and his grandfather. The picture of all of them in the same house—yes, a large Victorian, but not big enough for her and Connor—plagued her the whole time she got ready for bed. She would be near him all the time. That realization she couldn't squash long enough to rest her exhausted body and mind.

But what choice did she have? If her dad hadn't had a stroke that affected his ability to talk, he would never agree to coming to Dallas and staying with her. His house wouldn't be ready for weeks. And it would be hard to protect her father and try to solve who wanted him dead.

Okay, maybe she should consider staying at Mike's house when her father was released. Somehow she had to ignore how seeing Connor again played havoc with the fragile threads of her life. She was so close to all those threads snapping. From what the sheriff told her last night, he couldn't spare a twenty-four-hour guard detail for long and Connor was very good at his job. Sean was relieved Connor was helping him with the case.

The sight of Connor's black Jeep Cherokee, covered in dust and mud, coming around the corner halted her pacing. She moved to the curb and climbed into his vehicle when he came to a stop.

She hadn't even closed the door when he said, "What were you thinking? Standing outside like that?"

She slanted a look toward him. "What did you think? The killer would do a drive-by and shoot me?"

"First, you were advertising where you're staying by being out front. I know there aren't many hotels around here, but a little doubt wouldn't hurt for as long as you could manage. And second, we don't know what the assailant's going to do next. Yes, he could drive by and shoot you. Who knows? Why take the chance?"

"Good morning to you, too." She buckled her seat belt. "I'll try to remember that, but you forgot one important thing. I'm probably not the target. Yes, there's a slim chance, and we need to find that out, but more likely my father is. I gave it a lot of thought last night, and I believe that even more now."

He snorted and pulled away from the curb. "And Sean agrees. That's why there's a deputy at Sunny Meadows guarding his room."

"What made you so grumpy this morning?" Cara noted the clean interior, in stark contrast to the exterior of the Jeep.

"No sleep."

"Me neither."

"I don't like you staying at that hotel."

"Because you can't control the situation?"

"Yeah." The tension emanating off him decreased, and his hands loosened their tight grip on the steering wheel. "I kept expecting to get a call in the middle of the night telling me you were dead. It's that small chance it *could* be you I can't shake."

For a moment Connor sounded as if he cared what happened to her. The way she'd run out on him would challenge anyone's forgiveness. She'd been a chicken, so out of character, all those years ago when she'd left Clear Branch without seeing him again or telling him goodbye. She now realized why. If she had, she'd been afraid he would convince her to stay and give them a chance. She couldn't risk that because she would have regretted it. Maybe not right away but later. She'd needed to do what she'd done, in spite of what happened in Nzadi.

"I'm sorry, Connor."

His heavy sigh dissipated the silence. "Until we know who sent the bomb, it's best to think you and your dad are both in equal danger. I know you've been in dangerous situations and obviously made it through unscathed. Use those same skills and think before you do something here. Just in case."

Unscathed? Hardly. She was a wounded individual even if those wounds weren't visible. The hurt deep inside wouldn't leave her. She didn't even know how to begin healing. Had she done the right thing? Yes, she had saved her client, but others had been put in danger and one woman had died. It was as though the incident in Nzadi forced all her past horrific experiences to come crashing down on her and make her question the skills and instincts she'd honed from years of experience. Now she felt buried by them.

In the middle of all that, an image of her mother lying on her bed, lifeless, after taking sleeping pills on top of drinking several glasses of wine, ruined her composure. No, she couldn't deal with that on top of everything else. With determination she shoved that picture back into the dark recesses of her mind.

"I wasn't saying sorry about this morning," Cara finally said into the quiet. "I was talking about thirteen years ago. I shouldn't have left without saying a word to you. I was— wrong."

A tic in his jaw twitched. His grasp tightened around

the steering wheel as the silence lengthened. "I've accepted we aren't meant for each other."

"We were young and there were so many possibilities in front of us. I never wanted to look back and have regrets."

He pulled into the driveway of her father's home. "And you don't have any regrets?"

"Did I say I was naive, too?" She looked away, pretending a great interest in the handle as she thrust the door open. "Yes, I have regrets. I can't imagine going through life and not having them."

Thankfully he didn't ask her what regrets, or she was afraid she would break down in front of him and actually tell him. Because one of the biggest regrets was not having someone to share her life with. She felt so utterly alone. Living out of a suitcase and moving from assignment to assignment around the world wasn't conducive to having a long-term relationship. And she would never do what her father had done. Marry then leave a spouse home continuously as he covered breaking news in the United States, as well as other countries.

But even more so, she didn't think she was capable of committing to a lasting relationship because of what she'd witnessed in her parents' marriage. Her father had often been gone, and she was the one who dealt with her mother's loneliness and sorrow that he wasn't there. Her mom's grief had led to her suicide. Why couldn't Cara have been enough of a reason for her mother to want to live? Coming back had been such a mistake, she thought, staring at her childhood home.

Connor came around the front. "Are you ready for this?"

She nodded. Her throat closed at the sight of the destruction visible on the lawn, not really remembering it from yesterday. She'd walked through bombed buildings before and thought she knew what to expect until she entered her home and saw what the bomb had done. In this very foyer where she'd played as a young child with her dolls, there was little left she could recognize. In the dining room the table she'd placed the packages on was gone, blown to bits, some impaled as tiny stakes in the walls that remained. She glanced toward the boarded-up window, with slits of light leaking through to illuminate the room. The stench of dust and black powder clung to the house, refusing to release their hold.

Among the debris that was strewn about the floor so heavily that she couldn't tell if there was tile, hardwood or carpet beneath it, she picked out a few pieces of what would have been birthday presents. What if the bomb *hadn't* been the package that had been delivered right before the explosion?

"I've always assumed that the package that blew up was the one that had just arrived, Connor. What if it had been one of the other ones or something else? For all I know someone could have come in and put another gift among the pile. I didn't keep count. We know it was a pipe bomb from the fragments found, but everything has been destroyed, so how do we know exactly which package carried the bomb?"

Connor swung around and faced her. "Which again stresses that we don't know who the intended target was. We should know more about the bomb when the forensic report comes back. We do know the point of origin is the dining room table. ATF is good at their job."

She shook her head. "After this, I need to go see Dad at the rehabilitation center. He can't talk much and his hand isn't steady enough to write legibly, but maybe he can answer some simple questions." She wished she'd kept better tabs on her father's activities. She wasn't even sure she would ask the right questions.

"Do you remember what the deliveryman looked like? What company he was from? We still need to check into that. It's a possibility the last gift contained the bomb. It's our best lead at the moment."

She replayed the scene where she opened the door and took the present, then signed for it. "He had on a white shirt, but honestly I can't remember anything else. I was on my cell with my employer, and my concentration was on what she was saying." She closed her eyes and again tried to bring up an image of the man. "He was wearing a blue ball cap and blue shorts. Blond hair. He had on sunglasses and I couldn't see his eyes. That's all." She released a deep breath. "That doesn't say much for my observational skills. Usually they are much better than that. Do you think he's the guy?" Her shoulders slumped, the weight of what they were discussing—her father's life—crushing her. "This feels personal."

"We need to track down the deliveryman. I'll have Sean ask the neighbors specifically about seeing a vehicle at your house about that time, or a deliveryman. We'll explore every possibility."

"When I opened the last package, the present was wrapped in black paper. I thought someone used black paper as a joke because it was Dad's sixtieth birthday."

"What was on the outside of that box?"

"The return address was *Global Magazine,* so if that was where the bomb was, Dad has to be the target."

"Anyone can put any kind of return address on a package. I doubt a person would announce where they work after sending a bomb."

The tension in her shoulders intensified. "I know."

"Let's get what you came for, then visit your dad at Sunny Meadows."

"First, I'd like to check his home office. I haven't been in there since I came home." The memories of the room left a bad taste in her mouth. That was where her father would let her know how disappointed he was with her. In high school she'd been valedictorian, but he'd never said a word about it and certainly hadn't congratulated her. In fact, during her graduation, he'd been in Russia.

"Sean took your father's computer and files down to the station. There may be something in them that points to who might want him dead. Later you can help us go through them. Maybe we can even get your father's input."

"Dad encrypts his computer files. I might know a few of his passwords. His communication is limited, but I want him involved. He can at least answer yes and no questions."

"Good. That's a start."

"Dad has a safe. There might be hard copies of notes and files in there. I know the combination." That was one of the few things her father had ever shared with her. "That is, if he hasn't changed the code."

Connor swept his arm across his body. "After you."

As she picked her way toward the back of the house, a sense of loss inundated her. There was more damage than she'd thought. It would take weeks to restore the house to the way it was. Inside the office she stood by the entrance, remembering the last time she'd been in here. The day she'd left Clear Branch after she and her father had fought. Actually, more like had a screaming match. He'd rarely raised his voice to her. Usually he had always been cold, unemotional. That day he'd informed her yet again how disappointing she'd been to him, that she wasn't reaching her full potential.

The accusation resounded in her mind from thirteen years ago. "How can you throw your life away staying here and marrying a local? You were meant for more than that." Disillusionment had dripped off each of his words.

She'd stormed away from the house, from Clear Branch, to finish her senior year at college. She'd never told her father she'd already made the decision not to marry Connor, but not because she was meant for more or because he was a local. She hadn't been ready to settle down into marriage. At that time, she'd needed to fulfill her dream to see the world, as if that would finally be the connection between her and her dad. As if she would finally understand why her father was always gone and had little time for his family. As a child, she'd imagined traveling all over the world like her father, seeing the same places. What was it about the rest of the world that kept her father away? What was better than home and family?

"Cara?"

Connor's deep husky voice intruded into her thoughts. She blinked and focused on him and the concern in his expression.

"Are you all right?"

She tried to shrug away the emotions drenching her. She couldn't. Anger and even sadness at her father hugged her in a suffocating embrace. "I'm fine." She marched over to the safe covered by a portrait of her mother, a long-suffering woman who had died heartbroken during Cara's first year of college. "I don't understand why he kept this in here. He didn't love her." She swung the picture aside to reveal the safe and punched in the combination on the keypad. When she opened the safe, its empty contents surprised her. "Dad used to keep important documents in here. I guess he could have changed his habits, but this doesn't bode well."

"So someone could have come in here and broken into the safe? If that's so, we're talking about a person with a certain amount of skill or a top-notch accomplice because it doesn't look like it's been touched."

She turned at the same time Connor stepped closer. She collided into him. He steadied her, his hands on her arms branding her. His gaze captured hers and held it for a long moment; the thundering of her heart drowned out all common sense.

Why else would she wonder if he still kissed as good as he did when they were dating?

She pulled away from his grasp and hurried toward the exit. "Let me get my clothes and then we can leave."

"I'm going to check this room some more. It's beginning to look like someone may have been in here, which means the files we have might not be all of them."

A minute later Cara collapsed on the bed in her old childhood bedroom. She was too vulnerable. She should flee back to Dallas and let Connor and Sean figure everything out. But what if it wasn't really about her father? Besides, she'd never run from a fight since that day she left Clear Branch. She wasn't going to start now.

And even more importantly, if someone was after her father, she should be the one to protect him. She'd never be able to live with herself if she didn't take this assignment.

She flipped open her cell and called her boss. When Kyra came on the line, she told her what had happened in the past twenty-four hours. "I may be here longer than I thought. Will you let Mr. Richards know I'll contact him when my father is safe?" She couldn't deal with the guy from the State Department right now.

"Yes. Is there anything else I can do? Send someone to protect you and your father?"

"No, I have everything under control. We'll be all right." At least she hoped what she said was true. "But I appreciate the offer. There is something you can do for me. Although my father is most likely the target, I want to rule myself out totally. I've thought of three men who went to prison because of my testimony and actions. I'd like to know where they are. David Adams, Tom Phillips and Nelson Dickerson."

"I imagine both Adams and Dickerson are still in prison, but I'll check to make sure and give you a call. I think Phillips was released for good behavior. Again, I'll double-check."

"Thanks. If he's out, find out where he's been lately, if he's traveled to Washington, D.C., or Virginia."

"I'll do more than that. If he's around here, I'll pay him a visit."

That was what she was grateful for about her employer. Kyra went the extra mile for her employees. After promising Kyra she would keep her informed of what was going on, Cara pocketed her cell, grabbed her gun and holster and quickly threw her clothes into her one piece of luggage. She was coming out of her room when she met Connor in the hallway.

"I was getting worried about what was taking you so long." He took the suitcase from her.

"I called my boss and brought her up to speed."

"Okay." Connor weaved his way through the mess to the front entrance, a temporary makeshift door with a padded lock. "While we're driving, you can tell me about who you think might come after you. Did you make that list last night?"

Stepping out onto the porch, Cara waited until Connor secured the door before pulling out a sheet of hotel stationary and handing it to him. "I thought of three people. I'm having Kyra check to see if they are still in prison. If not, she'll find out where they are."

He tossed her suitcase onto the backseat, then opened the front passenger door for her before rounding the front of his Jeep and climbing inside. She was so used to doing everything for herself that the polite gesture took her by surprise. In the past he'd always made her feel like a lady. That part of him hadn't changed.

When Cara settled into the vehicle, she angled toward him. "Kyra says she heard Tom Phillips is out of prison, but she doesn't think the others are. She'll let me know for sure."

"Good. I'll do my own checking into these men." Connor backed out of the driveway and headed toward the edge of town where the rehabilitation center was, halfway between Clear Branch and Silver Creek.

"Out of those three, if I had to say who would come after me, I would say David Adams. He wasn't too happy with me after the conviction came down, but he was sent away for twenty years and even with good behavior he won't get out anytime soon."

"He could have paid someone to come after you." At a stop sign, Connor drummed his fingers on the steering wheel.

"I agree and could see that, but he didn't have any money left after paying for the lawyer. However, there are other ways to pay for a hit, and the look he gave me certainly said he would do what he could to make sure I wasn't around for long."

As he crossed the intersection, he gave her an assessing look. "You used to not be so cynical. What happened?"

"Life happened. I was young when I knew you before. I didn't know all about the evil there was in the big, wide world."

"Your father's articles and stories weren't a clue?"

"Reading about it is one thing. Living it is entirely different. People have constantly disappointed me in my line of work. How can you not say that, too? You're in law enforcement and you've most likely seen more horrific things than I have."

He stopped at a red light and slid his gaze to hers. "I have. There are times I haven't been sure I can continue. That's when I turn to the Lord for guidance and solace."

"How can He sit by and let evil exist?"

"The evil exists because people chose for it to. We have free will. We can give in to temptation or fight it." When the light turned green, he pressed on the accelerator. "I gather you have stopped going to church."

"It got harder and harder with traveling, and then the things I saw just overwhelmed me. I couldn't see praying to a God who let those things happen." She'd become tougher, but over the years her experiences had chipped away at that hard armor that held her emotions in check.

Connor pulled into a space in the parking lot next to the rehabilitation center wing of Sunny Meadows, turned the engine off, then shifted toward her. His gaze seized hers. "The Lord offers hope that there is a better way, but a person has to want to believe in that hope. He never guaranteed us an easy life, but He did guarantee us He would be with us always, loving us no matter what."

Is that what I need? She didn't know. Confusion had ruled in her ever since her time in Nzadi, Africa. She certainly didn't have much hope.

He took her hand on the seat between them and clasped it between both of his. "If you need someone to listen, I'm here. After my first year as a police officer in Richmond, I'd walked away from the Lord. I felt exactly like you.

But a fellow officer listened to me and helped me see the destructive path I was starting down."

The feel of his hands cocooning hers brought back all the happy times they'd had in the past. For a moment she wished she could go back to that time. But that wasn't reality. She tugged away and threw open the door.

He made her think that all she had to do was believe in the Lord and everything would be all right. Life wasn't like that. She strode toward the building. Or was it? That question niggled her mind as she entered Sunny Meadows and found her father's room with a young deputy outside the door. The sight of the officer brought relief to her, but she still wanted to find a safe place and bring her father there so she could protect him. Was that Connor's grandfather's house?

When Cara entered her father's room, he sat in an electric wheelchair, looking out the window. His arms lay listlessly in his lap with his shoulders hunched. The edges of his mouth turned down as though a permanent scowl etched his features. A curl of his jet-black hair contrasted with the pasty white of his face. He'd always loved the outdoors and to see him confined like this was painful. Maybe she could cheer him up. The last time she'd been here two days ago he'd been very agitated and upset as though seeing her brought to the foreground all the things he couldn't do anymore.

"Happy birthday, Dad. How are you today?" she asked in a forced tone of cheerfulness.

He glanced toward her, his gaze straying behind her. His eyes narrowed on Connor coming into the room. She didn't need to turn around to know that was who stepped through the doorway. A ping of awareness jolted her.

Her father faced forward, not looking at her, not looking out the window anymore, either. She drew in a fortifying breath and approached him. As she knelt in front of him to capture his attention, she winced at the pain caused by the action. Her sore hip plagued her but she couldn't give into it. She had too much to do.

"I'm sorry I wasn't here yesterday, but there was a lot to take care of after the bomb went off." He didn't need to know that she'd been hurt in the blast. When Sean had talked to him last night to explain about the deputy, he had assured her father that she was all right. She pasted a smile on as though her body didn't ache.

Agitation deepened the grooves on her dad's face. He tried to speak, but the words came out unintelligible. He curled his good hand into a fist.

"I understand that you're going to write your memoir. Have you started it?" Cara tried again to get some kind of response from her dad other than anger.

Her father shook his head slightly.

"I'm going to talk to the doctor about when he's going to release you. When he does, Mike Fitzgerald has offered to let us stay at his place until the house is restored. We'll celebrate your sixtieth birthday proper then." She decided not to say anything about the safe being empty until later. He didn't need more bad news after the shock of the bombing. He wasn't the tough man she'd become accustomed to over the years. Instead he was frail. Confused. Not in control.

A sound out in the corridor drew her and her father's attention. Connor stepped out of the entrance and pivoted toward the noise. A nurse's aide emerged with a large male orderly from the room across the hall. The young woman pushed a cart full of what appeared to be someone's personal belongings.

Her father groaned and tried to say something, but it came out in a garbled spew. He lifted his left arm, the one not affected as much by the stroke, and plopped it down onto Cara's shoulder.

"What's wrong?" she asked, alarmed at the look of panic in his eyes. Her father never used to panic. He'd always handled things calmly. The stroke had changed a lot for him. Made him feel vulnerable. And now the bombing had only reinforced that feeling.

Her dad managed to point toward the door with his left hand, but again she couldn't understand the words coming from his mouth. After a couple of attempts, he clamped his lips together, anger shooting from his eyes.

Strangely, Cara didn't feel the anger was directed at her. "Are you upset that the man across the hall died a couple of days ago?"

He blinked once for yes.

"Did you know him? Were you two friends?"

He shook his head, again only slightly. Frustration marked his expression.

Cara covered his hand in his lap. "I know this isn't easy for you. You're used to doing what you want when you want. I'm going to get you out of here as soon as Doc says I can." Seeing her dad so disturbed by the death of a stranger disconcerted her. His reaction reminded her of his behavior right after her mother had died. Which didn't really make any sense. He hadn't known the man across the hall. According to the nurses, her dad rarely left his room, preferring to be alone.

Her father tried to talk again. She still couldn't understand him. It was as if he conversed in a foreign language.

"Dad, do you want me to get some paper and pencil and see if you can write better today?"

He gave her a yes.

She retrieved the pad from the nightstand, her gaze

catching Connor's. Concern for her dad cloaked Connor's features, and yet her father had done nothing to deserve that. In fact, he had loudly disapproved of Connor when she was dating him. A warmth around her heart spread outward for Connor. She shouldn't let it grow and take over because they were worlds apart now.

As she gave her father the paper and pencil, even helping to place the writing instrument correctly in his hand, the orderly came back wheeling a gray-haired woman slumped in her chair, her chin nearly touching her chest. They went into the room across the hall.

"It looks like you'll have a new neighbor," she said, hoping to lift her father's spirits.

He gripped the pencil and painstakingly tried to write something. But since he was right-handed, the scrawl ended up in a jumbled mess. The only letters legible were *ger* at the end of what he wrote. In frustration, her father knocked the pencil to the floor.

"You didn't have to walk me to my room. The hotel is full of people and there are security cameras all over the place. I don't think anything is going to happen to me. Did you see the crowd in the lobby?" Cara stopped at her hotel room door.

"Don't play naive with me. You know good and well anything can happen in a crowd, including murder."

After the long, tiring day at the rehabilitation center then at the sheriff's and a contractor's, she hadn't wanted to argue with Connor. She wasn't even sure she could string a series of coherent sentences together to form an intelligent conversation. All through dinner at a diner, she'd hardly said anything. But then, neither had Connor.

"I know today wasn't easy for you. The C. J. Madison I knew wasn't like that man at Sunny Meadows. I figure he wasn't too happy for me to witness his lack of ability to communicate."

Not even an impromptu birthday celebration at the center with cake had brought a smile to her father's face. Birthdays had always been a big deal to him. "I think that may be the problem with me being there, too. He always seemed so powerful, in control, and to see him like this pains me. But I suspect it pains him more. Every time he has seen me he's been agitated. When I first visited him in the hospital right after the stroke, he wasn't very responsive and not really aware of too much. But now that he is, he's so angry, which is understandable, but hard to deal with." She expelled a long breath. "I understand from the speech therapist he won't recover his speech quickly and may always have some trouble communicating his thoughts, since the stroke affected the left side of his brain."

"Tell you what. I'll pick you up for breakfast tomorrow before you go to see your father, and we can go over what we have so far. I'm hoping some of the results will come back from the lab soon."

"Like what?"

"Maybe there's a fingerprint somewhere on one of the fragments from the pipe bomb. Also, there might be something on one of the pipe pieces that would identify the manufacturer." He stepped closer, touching her arm. "Cara, get some rest. You're father is safe right now. We'll figure this out together."

His words soothed her and gave her hope for the first time in days. "I'm hoping so. My dad's life may depend on it."

A fleeting emotion glittered in and out of his gaze so fast she couldn't read it. He moved in even closer, lifting his hand to cup her face. "I'm not going to let anything happen to you or your dad. That's a promise, Cara."

Her pulse pounded a quick rhythm. A few inches separated them. His scent swirled around her, binding her to him as though thirteen years hadn't passed.

But it had. She pulled back before she lost her heart to him again. In those years they had gone down different paths—miles apart. His faith had strengthened; hers had weakened until the threads threatened to sever completely.

"Tonight I'm going to get some sleep." She attempted a smile that failed. "At least I hope so." Cara slipped her keycard into the lock and opened her door. "Thanks for walking me to my room."

When she was inside, his words stopped her. "Let me check everything out."

She patted her gun in her holster at her side, saying, "I can do that." She held the door open wide so Connor could peek inside.

He stood in the entrance and made a visual survey of the area, then returned his full attention to Cara. "I know you can take care of yourself. You have been doing that for quite some time. But it's all right to let others help."

She shrugged, taking her suitcase from him. "Old habits are hard to break."

"Exactly, and the past is hard to run from. I'm discovering that. Good night. See you tomorrow at eight."

She closed the door and leaned back against it. Her eyes slid shut. Connor's image crowded her mind, his words replaying in her thoughts. *The past is hard to run from.* How well she knew that. She'd been running for thirteen years, and now the past was demanding she halt and face it. She needed to come to terms with Connor, but also with her mother's suicide and her relationship with her father. She needed to forgive her father for causing her mother to kill herself. He might as well have given her the alcohol and

sleeping pills. She took them because he was never around.
And when Cara went away to college that first year, she'd
no longer been around for her mother, either.

Pushing herself upright, she dragged herself toward her
bed, so exhausted all she removed was her jacket, dropping
it on the floor along with her suitcase. After taking her holster and gun off and placing them on the nightstand, she
collapsed onto the soft mattress, intending to regroup then
change into her pajamas. The events of the past thirty-six
hours crashed down on her, and she fell asleep as her head
touched the pillow....

*She ran into the rain forest, trying desperately to find
a hiding place. Stumbling, she went down on her knees,
falling forward. The scent of pine surrounded her. Pine?
In a jungle? When she rolled over, a weight pressed down
on her chest, making each breath difficult. Her oxygen-
starved lungs burned....*

Cara's eyes bolted open. In the dim light of her hotel
room, a looming figure clad in black and wearing a black
ski mask pinned her to her bed, straddling her. A leather-
gloved hand covered her mouth, trapping her scream inside
while he brought the other hand up toward her neck.

FOUR

The large, leather-clad hand squeezed around Cara's neck, cutting off her air supply. For a second or two she froze, her mind blank. A scent—like wet, sickly sweet pine—assailed her nostrils. Until he covered her nose as well as her mouth.

Then her instinct and training kicked in. She wouldn't go down without a fight. With her free arm, she plummeled at his back as she tried to twist from side to side. Anything to loosen his hold on her.

Bucking him, she managed to free her pinned arm and fumbled toward the nightstand. Searching for her gun. Desperation kicked her heartbeat up to a maddeningly fast tempo. Her mind spun from lack of oxygen. His dark form hovered.

Her fingers seized the alarm clock, and she quickly brought it down on his head. Over and over. His hand eased its tight grip as he shifted to grab her arm.

When he lifted up slightly, she rolled to the side, away from him, throwing him off balance. Again she brought the sturdy, heavy-duty clock down on him, this time smashing it into his face. A bellow of pain spewed from him; his hand slid from her mouth.

She screamed, but only a low choking sound came forth.

Her throat burned. Gulping in several deep breaths, she yelled "Help!" as loud as she could.

With a shove, she pushed him from her and clobbered him again with the clock before scrambling from the bed. She had to get to her gun on the nightstand on the other side. Halfway there, the light from the window illuminated the room enough that she could see the dark outline of her holster with the gun in it. But then he tackled her, sending her flying into the desk chair. A moan spilled from her as she kicked and hammered at him.

When her punch struck his Adam's apple, she found her chance to scoot across the carpet and reach up toward her gun. Inches away. Her fingers clutched the edge of the nightstand.

In a low, raspy voice, he said, "You'll pay for that."

Another scream came from deep inside her, so piercing she hoped the whole floor heard her.

Someone pounded on the door and rattled the handle. Her assailant jerked his head toward it. He leaped off her, raced toward the opened window and dove through it at the same time the door flew open. Light from the hallway poured into the room. Cara clambered to her feet as the man in the entrance flipped on the light.

She gasped. "Connor!"

With his gun drawn, Connor spied the open window and rushed to it, saying, "Are you okay?"

Cara barely got out the word *yes* before he plunged through the opening, the hot night air enveloping him. He heard the intruder clamor down the metal fire escape right outside Cara's room and descended it in pursuit.

When he neared the ground, he hopped the last four feet and hit the pavement running toward where he saw the man disappear around the corner of the hotel. Coming out of the alley into the back parking lot with security lamps providing illumination, Connor paused to scour the area for any sign of Cara's assailant.

Suddenly to the left, a car started and pulled out of a space. It was heading right toward him with its bright lights blinding him. He flung himself to the side, his body crashing into the hard asphalt. He scampered to his feet, ignoring the pain radiating from his palms, and stared at the vanishing vehicle. A white Ford Taurus with no license plate. Great.

His surge of adrenaline began to abate as he holstered his weapon and turned back to the fire escape. On his climb to Cara's room, he checked the area to see if the man had left anything, but the shadows of night obscured his search. Tomorrow he'd be back to investigate further.

Right now he needed to make sure Cara was all right. The sight of her on the floor near her bed, the clothing she wore that day still on but crumpled, a button torn off her shirt, increased his pace back to the fire escape. All his protective instincts came to the foreground, demanding he do something whether Cara liked it or not.

Memories of her trying to prove her worth to her father time and time again permeated his thoughts as he climbed to the second floor. She was going to accept his invitation if he had to hog-tie her and bring her to Gramps's house, protesting the whole way. And somehow he would make it work—seeing her every day until he could catch the person after her.

Stepping back through the open window, he panned the room for her. She wasn't there. A spike of fear pierced through his gut. Then he saw her coming out of the bathroom, her hair combed, her clothes straightened, her expression composed as though nothing had just happened in here only minutes before. But the red imprint of fingers around her neck proclaimed otherwise.

"Pack your things. You're coming home with me," he said in his gruff-sounding voice and immediately realized his mistake.

She drew herself up tall, her arms ramrods at her sides. One brow lifted. "I am?"

Sucking in a deep, calming breath, he tried to relax his tensed muscles but didn't succeed. Fear and anger still gripped him. "Yes." He waved his hand around the mess the fight with her assailant had caused. "You're many things, but stupid isn't one of them. It seems the man is after *you,* not your father. I know you're capable of taking care of yourself, but as I told you earlier, it's okay to accept help." He tempered his voice to a soothing level, hoping that would mollify her enough to come with him to his grandfather's house.

A hotel security officer stepped into the doorway, alert. He took a look at the scene before him and said, "Someone reported they heard a scream and a loud crashing sound. What's going on, ma'am?"

"I was attacked in my room, and this man came in to help me."

Before she could tell the guard who Connor was, he moved forward and withdrew his badge to show the man. "I need you to call Sheriff Taylor and report that Cara Madison was assaulted. I don't want anyone in here except the sheriff and his men."

"Yes, sir." The security officer squared his shoulders while reaching for his cell. "I'll take care of it. I'll stand guard and make sure no one comes in here until he arrives."

While the man planted himself outside the room in the

hallway and placed a call to Sean, Cara faced Connor. "Why are you here?"

He'd known she would ask, had expected he would have to counter her arguments about how she could take care of herself without him. Even thirteen years before, they'd argued about that. "I took the room next to yours tonight."

Her eyes widened. "You did? Why didn't you say something to me?"

"Because I didn't want to hear how you didn't need me to do that. Frankly, I was doing it for myself. I didn't sleep much last night, and I wanted a good night's sleep." He couldn't quite admit that he'd spent most of the night before worrying about her safety, although the implication was there in his answer.

"Did you see him flee the area?" She walked to the dresser and opened a drawer.

"Yes. He almost ran me down."

"A license number?"

"There was no plate. The car was a white Taurus, though, maybe a few years old."

"So we don't have much to go on." She delved into the drawer and grabbed the clothes she'd worn the day before—still dust covered with evidence of the bombing.

"We?"

She gave him an exasperated look as she packed her belongings in the suitcase. Rubbing her sore neck, she cleared her throat and said, "Yes. Remember we talked about figuring this out together? This is my life. My dad's. I have a vested interest in the outcome of this investigation."

When she closed her suitcase and started to lift it, he clasped her arm and stopped her. "I understand your need to compartmentalize yourself. To shut off your emotions and approach this in a calm way. I've certainly done my share of that working cases, but Cara, that man was going to kill you tonight."

The eyes that peered at him—for just a fleeting moment—held fear in them before she veiled her expression behind a neutral one. "If I panic, I could make a mistake. You know that. I can't afford to let my emotions take over. You might believe the man is after me, but I don't totally believe my father isn't the target. We need to look into both of us."

He grinned, but there was little humor behind it. "Sure. I'll look into your past. You can tackle your dad's."

She blinked. "I can investigate myself."

"You need an objective eye." His smile grew. "What's wrong? Do you have secrets you don't want me to know?"

She yanked her arm from his grasp. "Don't we all?" she said in a raspy voice as she picked up her luggage. "Are you ready?"

Surprised at how easy it had been to get her to leave the hotel, Connor stood in the middle of the room, not moving an inch.

"As you said, I'm not stupid. This place has been compromised. I wouldn't get any sleep staying here, and if I'm going to figure out who wants me dead, I need my rest."

The smile she sent him went straight through his heart, nudging open the lid on his past. It had taken years to get over her, and he wasn't going to go down that path again. They were not the same people they were as teenagers who fell in love. At least on his part. He wasn't sure Cara knew how to love, especially with her dad and mom as role models. In the past, she'd said the right words, but he'd always felt a reserve. Then she left him and Clear Branch without a goodbye. Even the letter she sent days later hadn't really explained her actions.

"Fine. I need to get my things from the room next door."

After he retrieved his small duffel bag and talked with the security man standing guard, he took out his cell and punched in a number. After five rings, Gramps answered and Connor said, "Cara has changed her mind. I'm bringing her to your house."

"I always said it's a good thing women like to change their minds."

Connor chuckled. "I wouldn't say that to her."

"Don't you worry about me. I'd say you're the one who's gonna have trouble."

Frowning, Connor slid his gaze toward the woman in question. "Nothing I can't handle." He clicked off and pocketed his phone. "Ready?"

She nodded and headed for the elevator.

After checking out, Connor paused at the back door that led to the parking lot behind the hotel. "You stay here. I'll bring the car to the front."

"You think he stayed around?"

"I don't know what to think. That's why we aren't sticking around for Sean. Why take the chance?" He pushed through the double doors and hurried toward his Jeep, scouting the area for anything unusual, especially a white Taurus.

Lord, I'm going to need You a lot over the next few days. Being around Cara is going to try my patience. I need to remain objective, emotionally distant. The woman I knew thirteen years ago isn't there anymore. I don't want to get pulled into her world any deeper.

Following the mouthwatering aroma of frying bacon and brewing coffee, Cara entered the kitchen, hoping to find only Mike. "You know how to get a gal to—"

The sight of Connor, alone, standing at the stove snapped her mouth closed on the rest of the sentence. He turned with a spatula in his hand and grinned. "Get a gal to do what?"

If the heat suffusing her face was any indication, she was blushing a deep shade of red. There was no way she would finish the sentence. She sauntered toward Connor, trying to resist the delicious smells coming from the skillet. But she loved fried anything, one of her weaknesses she had to fight constantly. "Can I put some water on for tea?" Although she enjoyed the scent of coffee, she much preferred tea if given a choice.

"Make yourself at home—" a few seconds pause then "—while you're staying here."

After putting some water on to boil, she went to the cabinet where Mike used to keep his tea bags and found them as though thirteen years hadn't passed. "Where's Mike?"

"Gramps went to get some groceries."

"When will he be back?"

"Why? Afraid to be alone with me?"

Cara stepped away a few paces, taking in Connor at the stove. He was wearing black jeans and a white T-shirt and no shoes or socks. His short dark brown hair, still wet from a shower, appeared as though he had combed it using only his fingers. "I was just wondering."

"Soon. Gramps would never miss a breakfast someone else cooked."

"Do you cook a lot?" The personal question came out unbidden. She wanted to snatch it back the second his gaze swung to her.

"I like good food, so yeah, I do. How about you?"

"Yes, when I get the chance, which isn't nearly enough. One of the disadvantages of being on the road a lot in my job." Although she hadn't meant to sound wistful, she did.

Connor slanted a questioning look her way as if trying

to figure her out. "Then I hope you'll cook us something while you're here."

"Sure. I want to pull my own weight. I'm not a guest."

"What are you then?" Connor removed the last piece of bacon and put it on the paper towel.

She cocked her head. "A friend?"

"But you aren't sure?"

"Not after how we parted all those years ago. I think we should talk about it. Get it out in the open so we can work together."

"Why? There's nothing really to talk about. You didn't want to get married. I did. That's pretty simple. I know now where we stand. Friends it is."

The dismissive way he spoke needled her as though what they had shared didn't mean much in the long haul. "Well, as a friend, what can I do to help with breakfast?"

"How would you like your eggs?"

"Over easy."

As he removed the carton of eggs from the refrigerator, he waved his hand toward the bread box. "You can make the toast. I'd like two pieces. Knowing Gramps, he will, too."

For the next few minutes she worked side by side with Connor in silence until his grandfather unlocked the back door and carried in two sacks of groceries.

"Connor, there's more in the truck."

Since the bread was in the toaster, Cara said, "I'll cook the eggs while you get the food."

When Connor left, Gramps strolled to the stove with a large mug and poured himself some coffee. "I'm glad to see you two haven't killed each other yet."

Cara chuckled. "We've come to an understanding of sorts."

"Yeah, it's the 'of sorts' that has me worried."

Not wanting to discuss Connor even with Mike, Cara flipped over the eggs in the skillet and asked, "Are you ready for my father? He was difficult before the stroke and now it's worse with his limitations."

"Don't worry about me, child. We need to focus on you and your dad and keeping y'all safe."

"But you don't understand. You haven't been around my father much. This stroke has really set him back. He's always been so active and articulate. Words have been a weapon he used with skill and cunning against his target, and now without the ability to communicate his thoughts, to him he's defenseless."

"In other words, he's angry and lashing out."

She nodded as she slid the eggs onto the plates on the counter.

"I can deal with him. My own father had a stroke. I took care of him. I understand what he's facing with his recovery. Your dad's attitude is the least of your worries."

She leaned back against the counter. "I know."

The back door opened and Connor came into the kitchen with three more bags. "Did you buy out the grocery store?"

"Practically. Next time I'll have to go to Silver Creek." Mike took a sip of his coffee. "You two go on and eat while I put away the groceries."

"But we can help." Cara started to empty the sack nearest her.

Mike stopped her with a hand on her arm. "I know where things go. I'm tolerating my grandson messing up my kitchen with his cooking, but that's where I draw the line. I'll have to live here after y'all leave, and I want to know where everything is. Sit and eat."

"Yes, sir," she said with a huge grin. "I'd forgotten how bossy you can be. I think you'll be just fine with Dad."

Connor brought their plates to the table. "Speaking of your father, when does he get to leave Sunny Meadows?"

"I'm hoping today, but it'll all depend on if Doc thinks his new medication is all right. I'll feel better when he's here where I can keep an eye on him better." Cara brought the platter of toast and set it between their place mats, then took her seat.

Connor bowed his head and said a quick blessing. Cara stared at the top of his head for a few seconds and then murmured, "Amen."

"We need to meet Sean at the hotel after we eat. I called him while I was cooking to see what he found last night. He wants you to tell him what happened. They processed what they could in the room but haven't touched the fire escape yet."

"Did they find anything?"

Connor shook his head. "A whole slew of fingerprints but since the man wore gloves they won't help."

"I need to see Dad." The whole mess gave her a feeling of urgency as though time was ticking down quickly.

"I'll take you to Sunny Meadows after we see Sean. We'll pick up your car at the hotel on the way back here later in the day."

"I also need to go by the house to meet with the contractor."

Mike took a chair across from her. "Who's working on your house?"

"Ned Morris."

"He's good and honest. He goes to my church." Mike grabbed a piece of toast and slathered on some strawberry jam. "Now let's talk about what we really need to discuss. Who wants you dead, Cara?"

"The only ones are David Adams, Tom Phillips and

Nelson Dickerson. Two I believe are still in prison. I think Phillips has been released."

"While you two are out gallivanting around, I'll do some checking on that trio of suspects."

"How?" Cara cut up her two eggs and ate a bite.

"Child, I am quite good with a computer. I may be old, but I keep up with the times."

"You should see him on it," Connor said with a laugh. "Once I set it up and taught him a few things, he took over and is probably better than I am at finding things."

"Since my boss is looking into those guys already, why don't you delve into the stories my father has written this past year, especially the last few months."

"Sure. By the end of the day, I'll know your father's stories inside and out. Then if I have time left over I'll tinker around in those three guys' lives. It doesn't hurt for me to check some of the social media sites for them. You can find out some interesting details about people on those sites that might help in the investigation."

Cara looked from Mike to Connor. "Who took over your grandfather? Wasn't he the man who didn't want you to go into law enforcement and tried to talk you out of getting a degree in criminal justice?"

"We came to an understanding thirteen years ago when I told him I was going to pursue my dream and follow in my father's footsteps. I couldn't see me staying here and taking over running Gramps's gas stations. I guess it took you leaving to make that clear to me. I reevaluated my life, quit my job at Gramps's and went back to college. You weren't the only one who wanted to do more than what was in Clear Branch."

"But you never said anything." His dad had been a state trooper who had died on the job. The idea that Connor and Mike had come to an understanding about his future made her long for that with her own father. But then Mike had always accepted Connor for who he was.

"That was the time one of my friends got hurt seriously in a tractor accident," Mike said. "I came to the conclusion danger could come from anywhere. That we can't live our life in fear of what might happen. I told Connor he needed to do what would make him happy."

What would make her happy? If only her father had urged her to do what she'd wanted. Long ago she'd given up the dream of having a family. She didn't know what that word really meant. She certainly couldn't go by the one she'd grown up in. She was destined to be alone, and she'd come to accept that. But there were times she was lonely.

"Have any of the tests on the bomb fragments come back yet?" Cara sipped her tea.

"That's a question we'll ask Sean when we meet him at the hotel in—" Connor peered at the clock on the kitchen wall "—fifteen minutes."

"Then we better get moving." Cara left the rest of the tea but quickly finished the last bite of her eggs and grabbed a piece of buttered toast to take with her. "I'll get my purse and call Sunny Meadows to see how Dad did last night. I can be ready in five minutes."

She rose and took her dishes to the sink. She started to rinse them when Mike stopped her.

"Child, you've got enough to do today. Don't worry about cleaning up."

She kissed Mike on the cheek. "I've missed you."

Mike peered over his shoulder to check if Connor had left the kitchen to finish getting ready, then looked back at her. "But not my grandson?"

Glad Connor was gone, she murmured, "Of course," then fled to her room before Mike questioned her about her feelings.

Ten minutes later, she stood on the back stoop and ate the last bit of toast while she listened to a bird sing in a nearby oak tree. *Tranquil* came to mind as her gaze swept over the yard that stretched back several acres. A riot of wild rosebushes along one fence offered a glimpse of beauty that she rarely took time to enjoy. Inhaling a deep breath of the sweet-smelling air, she sighed. For just a moment she could imagine that someone wasn't after her and all was well with the world.

"What are you doing out here in plain view for anyone to see you?"

The thunder in Connor's voice dissipated the serenity. She knew he was right. She had cautioned many clients about exposing themselves unnecessarily, and yet the summer day had drawn her outside. Not yet hot with just a hint of crispness from the evening before, the morning was gorgeous.

"For once, I wasn't thinking."

"That could get you killed. Something I shouldn't have to remind you of after last night's attack. I didn't think I had to tell you that." His mouth firmed into a scowl as he descended the steps, shifted around and waited for her.

"A moment of folly that won't happen again."

His frown dissolved into a bland expression. "I don't want to see anything happen to you or your dad."

"After how my father treated you, I'm surprised you feel that way." She started for his vehicle.

"I forgave him long ago."

Cara came to a halt and faced Connor. "You forgave him? He did everything to keep us apart. He was rude and belittled you. There wasn't anything you could do to please him."

"Holding a grudge against him was doing me more harm than he was. He wouldn't even know it, but I would have to live with that kind of hate each day. Besides, his action goaded me into making something of myself."

She snapped her fingers. "So just like that you forgave him?"

"It wasn't quite that easy, but I actually feel sorry for your father. I don't think he's a very happy man."

"Yeah, he had a stroke that has curtailed all his activities."

"No, way before that. I saw him in town a couple of years ago. We spoke. He was civil, but I saw something in his eyes that gave me pause."

Cara climbed inside the Jeep. "What?"

"Loneliness."

Her father had a ton of friends who he'd worked with over the years. She remembered all the birthday presents piled up on the dining room table before the explosion. But on the short drive to the hotel, she couldn't shake the possibility of her father being lonely. He'd always come across as though he needed no one in his life to complete it—not even her or her mother.

At the hotel Connor parked close to the back entrance. "I didn't see anyone following us so it should be safe. Wait, though, until I open your door." He exited and scouted the area before rounding the front of his SUV to the passenger side.

Seconds later they entered the hotel. Cara got a taste of being on the other end of her job. She was the client, Connor the bodyguard.

The sheriff was waiting in the lobby. "How are you holding up, Cara?"

"I've had better days."

"The security guard told me they would put a new door on the room after I processed the scene last night. I've got the key." Sean punched the elevator button, and the doors immediately swished open.

When they reached the room, Sean said, "It looks like you put up quite a fight."

Scanning the scene of the crime as an observer, Cara noted the overturned wastebasket and didn't even remember hitting it. The bed covers were askew with part of the bedspread on the floor. The desk chair was knocked on its side. A shiver flashed down her spine, causing goose bumps to prick her arms. For a few seconds, she relived the feel of her attacker's hands on her neck. The suffocating sensation. The fear. The desire to live.

"Tell us what happened," Sean said as Connor walked to the window, closed now.

She vaguely remembered him shutting it when he came back up the fire escape. Now she noticed where the glass had been cut. The intruder must have then reached in and unlocked the window.

"I woke up with a man on me. He put his hand over my mouth and the other one around my neck. That's when I started fighting. I managed to get hold of the clock and clobber him a few times with it." Again the sensation of being choked overwhelmed her until she determinedly shut it down. Nothing would be accomplished by reliving it.

"Did he say anything?" Connor asked after raising the window.

She replayed the scene in her mind, this time with her emotions in check. Almost as though she were an observer. "Something about 'I'd pay for what I did.'"

"What was he talking about?" Sean walked toward Connor.

"I punched him in the Adam's apple. He didn't appreciate that."

"Do you see what I see?" Connor pointed outside.

Cara covered the distance to them and peered between the two men. A dried, dark splotch marred the metal grid of the landing. Blood? "Do you think it's the assailant's?"

"Maybe," Sean said, wetting a swab with sterile water before rubbing it across the stain. Then he squeezed a drop from several bottles of solution onto the swab. When the tip of the swab turned pink, he put it in an evidence bag. "This alone couldn't convict anyone, but it sure would be nice if we can find a DNA match in the system. It's evidence that puts the person at the hotel." He climbed through the opening to collect a sample of the dry, red-crusted stain.

"Any good lawyer would say it could have been left anytime." Connor shifted around to survey the room again.

"We had a downpour the other night, which probably narrows the timeline some." Sean pocketed the evidence. "I'm going down this way. I'll meet you two below."

Cara closed the window, wanting to get out of the room. She'd been involved in some harrowing experiences but she'd never been the intended target.

"Did you draw blood?" Connor asked from the entrance into the room.

"I don't know. It was dark and all I was thinking about was getting away from him. I hit him several times with the alarm clock. That could have bled. I remember striking at his head. Maybe I connected with his face. Bloodied his nose or something."

He glanced where the clock would normally sit. "It looks like Sean took it as evidence. I didn't notice any blood on you. It's likely he would have had blood on his gloves from wiping at his face."

"I didn't have any, so the blood on the railing might not have been from our guy."

Connor stepped out in the hall and waited for Cara. "I

can get the sample to our lab, but it'll be several weeks before we hear back."

"Several weeks?"

"Yeah, and that's when I call in a favor. There's a backlog, and it doesn't happen as fast as it does on TV."

Downstairs in the alley next to the hotel, Sean and Connor checked the ground below the fire escape. There were a few cigarette butts and a candy wrapper, which Sean bagged. Connor found a couple of drops of blood and went up the ladder to the second floor where her room was.

He leaned over the railing and said, "I think I see what happened. A piece of metal on the railing is sticking out, and I think our assailant might have cut himself on it. At least let's hope so."

Connor descended to the ground. He and Sean began to follow the trail of blood down the alley toward the back parking lot. The dried drops led to a parking space in the first row near the alleyway. "This is where the car came from that tried to run me down, so this blood is probably from our guy. I noticed the clock wasn't in the room. Did you take it for evidence?"

Sean nodded. "Yes, but I didn't see any blood on it. It was obvious it had been used in the fight, though, so I'm having the lab check it out."

Cara scouted the area, wondering if he was out there watching her right now. The sensation that she was the target chilled her and gave her even more insight into how her clients felt. Had the trophy wife in Nzadi felt this way? Hidden her fear behind a false bravado? Even with her training, Cara couldn't stem the apprehension enveloping her.

Connor must have sensed what was going on in her head because he approached her, touching her arm briefly as though to reassure her he was there. "We have a lead. That's a step forward."

She attempted a smile, wishing she could dismiss the anxiety gripping her. She couldn't. Connor's help and presence, though, made her feel she wasn't totally alone in dealing with this. The realization brought her comfort.

Sean's cell rang and he answered it. After a minute, he replied, "Good. I'll tell Connor. He's here with me." When he hung up, he turned toward them. "The analysis of the bomb came back. There's a fingerprint on one of the pipe pieces. Eddie King's. He owns King Construction Company in Silver Creek. They use blasting powder, too."

"Great. I'll check him out if that's all right with you after we see Cara's dad at Sunny Meadows."

"Yes, I'm stretched thin as it is with keeping a deputy on C.J. You know how hectic things can get around here near Labor Day. The last fling of summer."

"I'll let you know what I find out."

"I'm sending the evidence to the state lab and will continue tracking down the person who delivered that last present to the door. We'll talk later." Sean nodded at Cara and strolled toward his patrol car.

"Ready, Cara?" Connor withdrew his keys and punched the unlock button. "You don't know an Eddie King by any chance?"

"No, but I'd like to see what he looks like. Names can be changed."

"So can faces."

"Not as easily." Cara slipped into the passenger seat.

Fifteen minutes later, they arrived at Sunny Meadows. Cara dreaded seeing her father. Her visits only agitated him, reinforcing their prior relationship.

When she entered the building, the sickly stench of the place roiled her stomach. At least she had a question to ask her dad. What if he knew Eddie King or had some dealings with the man? She hadn't totally ruled out her father as the main target—not with his ability to anger some powerful people with his investigative reporting. Whoever tried to kill her last night might have come after her because she was a witness—and survivor—of the bombing.

They were both targets.

FIVE

At her father's room Cara came to a stop a few feet inside. Doc Sims finished pressing on her father's stomach. Her dad grimaced and said something she didn't understand, but the anger behind the sound was evident. Doc's gaze swung to hers, concern etched on the man's face.

Cara approached Doc. "What's wrong?"

He moved a few paces away from the bed and lowered his voice. "I don't know. This second medicine isn't agreeing with him, either. I don't like that yellow tint to his skin, which means his liver is involved. I'm running some tests. He's complaining of stomach problems and has been nauseated. I'm going to switch to another medication and hope this one works."

A guttural sound emitted from her father as he pounded his fist on the bedding next to him. Anger carved deep lines into his gaunt face.

Cara hurried to him. "Dad? Are you in pain?"

He shook his head but kept hitting his balled hand into the covers bunched up around him. Another low sound— that could be the word *no*—came from his mouth.

Cara tried to touch his arm to calm him down but he knocked her hand away.

Doc moved in between her and her father. "Maybe you should step outside. Get the nurse."

Trembling, Cara did as the doctor asked then waited out in the hallway. She collapsed against the wall and hugged her arms across her front. The stress of yet again being rejected by her dad wrapped about her and squeezed, making her breathing difficult. All she wanted to do was help him. But he couldn't accept that.

Connor parked himself next to her while he surveyed the activity going on around them. "I'm sorry, Cara."

"What's happening to Dad? He'd always been difficult, but this is different."

"A major dose of frustration?"

"Maybe. I thought he was making good progress. Learning to use his left hand to write. Even making a few words recognizable when he tried to communicate, especially when he didn't get upset. When his speech and occupational therapists talked with him, he seemed to understand it would take time to regain his abilities."

"This latest setback might be the last straw. The man in there was used to uncovering crime and corruption in many places others weren't able. He's the one who broke the case against that CEO for Bakers and Stevens Financial a couple of years ago and that crime syndicate in Maryland was finally taken down because of his investigation."

"I know. Just recently he took on a powerful federal judge who had to step down from the bench because of Dad's story." Her father had always fought for justice in his own way and helped a lot of people in the process. Why couldn't their relationship be better? Why was he there for others, but not her?

"What else has he done this past year? I know Gramps is looking into it, but what do you remember?"

"The head of that gang in Washington, D.C., was

brought to trial for murder, along with his second in command, and this time there should be a conviction. Dad's informant gave him the information he needed to make that happen." Cara angled toward Connor, her shoulder cushioned against the wall. "Now you see why I think Dad could still be the target. He's done a lot to anger some powerful people over his career."

"True, and we're still going to look into his past stories, starting with the most recent ones. But we can't dismiss the attack on you last night."

The door to her father's room opened, and the older man who had been the family doctor ever since Cara could remember exited. His gaze lit upon her. He stopped in front of her, a frown on his face.

"I've had to sedate him. We're checking his liver function and we'll keep a close eye on him. He'll be out for a while. Why don't you come back later? Hopefully he'll be calmer by then. Maybe I'll have some answers about what's going on."

Cara glanced at the door then at the deputy standing next to it. "Fine. The nurses' station has my cell if you need to get ahold of me."

When she started to walk away, Doc said, "Anger and frustration are something I've seen before in cases like this. It's not that unusual, Cara. Remember, people often strike back at the ones closest to them."

Yeah, she'd tried to console herself with that before, but she'd come to the end of her tolerance. She needed more. She would see her father settled in at home with the care he needed, but after that she would leave Clear Branch. Of course, that was after the renovation of the house and once the person who had sent the bomb was caught.

Doc settled his hand on her shoulder. "It'll take time for your father to adjust to his limitations."

"Limitations? You have known Dad long enough to know he'll never adjust to anything less than full recovery."

"He may have to." Doc patted her arm. "You've done what you can. Let me see what I can come up with."

On the way out of the building, Cara fought to boost her spirits, but the sight of her dad shouting and striking the bed played across her mind over and over. She didn't even realize she'd slowed her pace until Connor peered at her and stopped.

"Doc will figure out what's going on and get your dad on the right medication."

"He has always been so strong. Seeing him that way is devastating. We never got along well, but I never wanted this for him." Brick by brick her life was crumbling around her. She didn't know if she wanted to continue working as a bodyguard. Being around Connor was more difficult than she could imagine. She'd hurt him thirteen years ago. His emotional distance was understandable, but she realized she didn't want it. She needed to be held, but she wouldn't ask him. She didn't know if she could do this alone and that was the most troubling of everything happening.

He held her hands between them, the slate gray of his eyes mesmerizing as he drew a few inches closer. "I'll help any way I can. Just let me know what."

The tears she needed to shed clogged her throat. She tried to push them back down, but the loneliness her life had become overwhelmed her. "Hold me," she murmured the words she hadn't wanted to say to him.

Without hesitation he pulled her against him, his arms encircling her. Being in his embrace felt as though she'd come home. Memories flooded her, and for a brief moment she wanted to surrender to the past.

But was that wise with all that was happening? Even

before coming to Clear Branch and the explosion, her life had been in an upheaval. She wouldn't hurt Connor again. She owed him that.

Backing away from the comfort of his arms, she smiled, only managing to hold it for a second. "Thanks. If I'm going to get my life back, we need to figure out what's going on, so let's go talk to Eddie King."

His eyelids sweeping down, he turned from her. "I *was* thinking of leaving you here with your father so that the deputy could protect you both while I went to Silver Creek."

"I'm coming with you. I have a stake in this investigation."

"I'm taking you with me, but that isn't the reason." He strode toward his SUV. "I'm afraid if I leave you here in Clear Branch you'd go off and do something you shouldn't."

She laughed, pointing at herself. "Me?"

"Yes, you." His gaze captured hers over the roof of his vehicle.

"Okay, maybe I would have, but I'll promise you right now that I won't go off and do my own investigating. If you leave me somewhere, I'll stay." She climbed in at the same time he did. "Does that make you feel better?"

He eyed her, a frown tugging at the corners of his mouth. "What have you done with Cara?"

"She's in here." She tapped her chest. "I figure since you're helping me the least I can do is not cause you any extra worry."

His laughter filled the Jeep's interior. "This is a day for the record books."

For a moment she joined him, merriment welling up in her and soothing her troubled mind. Connor could always make her laugh. She'd forgotten about that.

* * *

Cara's silence worried Connor as they drove to King Construction in Silver Creek. If this didn't pan out, there were other leads; the type of pipe used in the bombing had been sold to several other companies in the state. But this was the nearest one and Eddie King's fingerprint had been lifted from inside a piece of the pipe. King didn't have a criminal record; a match had come up in the database because he'd served in the army, so his prints were on record. King Construction had also ordered some blasting powder a few weeks ago. This had to be the source.

He pulled into the parking space in front of King Construction's headquarters, a one-story building on the edge of Silver Creek's downtown. Behind the office was a larger structure that appeared to house equipment and supplies, and a smaller one next to it. Was that where the black powder was kept? It made sense to keep it in a separate building.

"I noticed you watching the traffic. No one followed us." Connor switched off his vehicle.

"It's a habit of mine. I find myself doing it even when I'm not working." Her gaze linked with his. "But I'm on a job. If I can't keep myself safe, then how can I keep anyone else safe?"

"Maybe Eddie King is the guy and we'll put this to rest."

"My gut says no. I did a search on my phone on the way here, and there are no ties with Dad or me. My father hasn't investigated the construction industry lately."

"It could be someone who works here."

"I know. I just don't think it'll be that easy."

The discouragement in her voice tugged at him. He wanted to reassure her but she was probably right. Some cases just fell into place. This didn't feel like one of them.

"Let's go. You know the drill. Stay in the car until I come around," he said as he climbed out.

When he reached the passenger door and opened it, Cara's tired expression had transformed into an unreadable one, which was often her facade even as a teenager when they were dating. He'd always suspected she'd learned to hide her feelings behind a mask because of her relationship with her father. In the past few days, especially in the parking lot at Sunny Meadows earlier, he'd seen more emotion on her face than usual. The events of the last few days were really taking a toll on Cara, but was there more to her state of mind than having an assailant after her, her father or both of them? He couldn't shake the feeling there was.

Inside the building Connor greeted the receptionist and showed her his ID and badge, noting, as cops did, her plain features, medium brown hair, brown eyes. A tattoo of an orange and black butterfly on her arm caught his attention for a few seconds before he said, "I'm here to see Eddie King. Is he here?"

The young woman's eyes grew round. She checked Connor's ID a second time and nodded.

"In his office?"

"No, in the warehouse out back." The woman's voice squeaked on the last word.

"Would you show us where?"

She bolted to her feet, smoothing down her short-sleeved dress. "This way."

Connor and Cara followed the receptionist out the back door and across an asphalted parking area. When they entered the cavernous building, he immediately scanned the inside of the structure, noting the machinery, stacked wood and any rooms off the larger one, where the exits were.

The receptionist stopped a few feet from the main

entrance and waved her hand toward a large man, approx-
imately two hundred and fifty pounds, six and a half feet
tall. "Mr. King is over there. I have to get back to the
phones."

"His build doesn't fit the man who attacked me," Cara
said after the receptionist left. "My assailant was maybe a
hundred seventy or eighty."

"No, but that doesn't mean he isn't involved in some
way. He'll need to explain why his fingerprint was on the
pipe used."

"Maybe he went to the manufacturer and handled it
there. Remington-Burke Industries isn't too far from here.
That's his supplier."

"I'll check with them if I need to. If this isn't the place,
the next nearest company that bought that piping from the
manufacturer is in Richmond. We'll check all of them if
we have to. The other two fingerprints on the pipe fragments aren't in the system. This is the only one we have
to go on."

Cara sighed, running her fingers through her short
russet-colored hair. "I can see why you went into law enforcement."

"Why?" he asked, curious about her take.

"You always loved a good challenge, and I remember
the harder the puzzle, the more you liked it."

"I still do. But the main reason was that I wanted to
make a difference in people's lives." He started forward,
casually putting his hand at the small of her back—like he
used to in the past.

King looked toward them as they approached, his gaze
narrowing, assessing. "What can I do for you?"

The smile on his face contradicted his voice, which held
a touch of wariness. Connor showed him his ID and said,
"I have some questions about some piping you ordered

from Remington-Burke Industries. Also some blasting powder you recently purchased."

A worker on the far side of the warehouse switched on a power saw.

King pointed toward a door a few feet away. "Let's go in here where it's quieter." In the small room with boxes stacked around its perimeter, he continued, "What questions?"

"You received a shipment of piping a month ago from Remington-Burke."

"Yes. What's this all about?"

"One consistent with what you purchased was used in a pipe bomb recently. Are you missing any in your inventory?"

"Don't know. Let me have my foreman check for you. He keeps track of that sort of thing." King went out into the main part of the building, leaving the door open.

The sound of the saw reverberated through the room. The scent of wood permeated the air, reminding Connor of his last camping trip into the Smoky Mountains. This vacation wasn't exactly turning out like that one.

Cara leaned back against a stack of boxes, folding her arms across her chest, dropping her head as she stared at the concrete floor.

There was so much he wanted to say to her, but he couldn't move. The feel of her in his embrace still lingered and so did the danger of getting too close to her emotionally. They weren't the same two people. He didn't really know this Cara.

When King returned a few minutes later, closing the door, a frown beetled his brow. "Vance checked the inventory, and there are two pipes missing."

Cara brought her head up, straightening away from the boxes. "When did that happen?"

King looked toward her. "He takes inventory every week and would have later today. Last week the pipes were there."

"How about your blasting powder? You bought it two weeks ago. Where is it?" Connor's question drew King's attention back to him.

"I use it on my construction sites occasionally. All legal."

"Can you account for all of it?"

"I'm sure I can. I haven't used any yet. We were supposed to last week, but the rain delayed us, throwing that project off schedule."

"Can you show me where it is? Blasting powder was used in the pipe bomb. A fingerprint was found on a fragment of the pipe used. It was yours."

King's face went white. "I check all orders that come in so that wouldn't be that unusual." He drew himself up taller, his gaze slipping to Cara briefly. "I assure you any explosives I use are kept under lock and key."

"Have you checked it lately?" Connor asked over the muted sound of the power saw.

"Well, not personally, since I put it in the shed."

"Please do to make sure you have it all. Unless there is some reason you don't want to." Connor kept his gaze on the man.

"No. No. I'll show you, and you'll see for yourself." King withdrew a set of keys and exited the room. Outside he stopped in front of the smaller building next to the warehouse and unlocked the door. He waved both Connor and Cara to go ahead of him into the shed.

"That's okay. After you." Connor stopped Cara from moving through the entrance until the owner went inside. He leaned close and whispered, "I gather he doesn't look familiar to you."

"Nope."

"The blasting powder is kept over here." King halted and lifted the lid on the box. A frown descended. The man glanced from side to side at the cartons lined up against the wall. "Part of it is missing, too." The pasty-white color returned to his face as the implication sunk in.

Connor examined the container King had. There was enough blasting powder missing for more than one pipe bomb. "Who has access to this place?"

"My foreman, Vance Dodson. But I store other things in here, and there's a key kept in my office desk drawer in case something is needed and one of us isn't around. But anyone would have to go through my receptionist to get the key."

"I need you to see if that key is there. If anyone has checked it out in the past week."

"Sure. I promise you I'll get to the bottom of this." King marched toward the exit, waited for Connor and Cara to leave, then secured the door. "I'll be changing the lock today."

"I assure you, *I'll* get to the bottom of it." Connor told the man as he again surveyed the area. A middle-aged man chewing a piece of gum watched them trek toward the entrance into the front building, the same man who King had left the room earlier to talk to. "How long has your foreman been working for you?"

"He wouldn't take the pipe or powder. He's been with me from almost the beginning."

When they entered King's office, he went directly to his desk and opened a top drawer on the left. "It's right here."

Not locked. "How easy is it to get the key from your desk?"

King cocked his head and stared off into space for a

good minute. "Like I said, a person has to check it out, but I guess pretty easy. Lucy is usually at her desk out front, but she does run errands for me and stuff like that. Not to mention she always goes to lunch between twelve and one. She has to go home and let her horde of dogs outside."

"Do people know about this key?" Connor walked toward a door on the other side of the room.

"Yes, probably. It's never really been a secret."

Connor gestured toward the door. "What's in here?"

"It's an exit."

"Is it usually locked?"

"Yes."

"I'd like a list of employees, including those who no longer work here, but did during the last few months."

King sat at his desk and pulled something up on his computer then hit the print button. "This is a list of current employees. I haven't let anyone go since early summer." Swiveling his chair around, he grabbed the sheet then gave it to Connor. "I'll get their names."

"Thanks, I may have other questions for you later. For the future, please secure your explosive materials better."

"So you think someone used the pipe and blasting powder from here to make a bomb?"

"It's looking that way. If not, you still have some missing. Either way, it isn't a good situation."

King nodded. "I agree. I've just been lucky and not had much stolen around here. I've let my security get lax."

On the way out, Connor paused at the receptionist's desk. "Lucy, has anyone checked out the key for the storeroom in the warehouse in the past two weeks?"

The young woman peered at her boss then back at Connor. "Let me check." She opened a side drawer and withdrew a notebook. "No. George was the last one three weeks ago."

As Connor and Cara left the building, he again inspected the terrain. "King said he checked inventory last week, but that doesn't mean he's not lying. Or that he and the foreman aren't in this together. The pipe and powder came from here."

"Yeah, especially since King's fingerprint was found on it, but who took them?"

"King was right about his security being lax. Anyone with a little knowledge could pick that lock on that other exit in his office. We'll need to look into the current and former employees. I'll have Gramps do that, as well as an agent at the main office in Richmond."

Cara smiled. "I can't get over the image of Gramps sitting in front of a computer for hours and enjoying it. He used to spend so much time outside."

"Yeah, and he still does that. He loves his flower and vegetable gardens, but when he's not out there tending to them, he's usually at the computer. He has friends all over the world. He keeps telling me he's going to go see a few of them, but I don't think he will. He's a homebody."

"Like you?"

"I guess. I don't stray far from Virginia." He opened the passenger door for Cara. "How did you do it? Travel from place to place. Never home much except to wash your clothes before going back on the road."

"I looked at it as an adventure each time I went out on an assignment as an investigative reporter, and later as a bodyguard."

"And you never got homesick?"

A shadow darted in then out of her gaze. She glanced away. He shut the door, rounded his Jeep and climbed behind the steering wheel.

He slanted a look toward her. "What happened in Nzadi?"

He'd heard rumors and seen the reports of the rioting at the time she'd left the country.

Her eyelids slid closed, and she rested her head back on the seat cushion. For a long moment silence reigned in the car.

When she reestablished visual contact with him, a bleak expression had taken hold in her gaze. "I learned how quickly my life could change."

He started the engine. Question after question floated through his mind. But in the end he only wanted to ask her: *Was seeing the world worth leaving me?*

"For you. Clear Branch held happy memories because it was your home but not mine—not really. It was a place where I grew up, but that's all. I couldn't wait to get away."

"Away from your dad?" *From me?*

"Yeah, but at the time I wouldn't have said that. I thought I was fulfilling my dream by traveling—seeing all the places my father had gone, experiencing what he did. I thought that might make me understand him better. I was wrong. I couldn't recreate his life in order to get his approval. It took tragedy in Nzadi to finally hammer that into my stubborn brain."

Connor chuckled. "Stubborn? You? No way."

Her gaze connected with his. "We both know I was." One corner of her mouth hitched up. "Still am."

He lifted his eyebrows. "You are?"

What light had entered her eyes vanished and her expression sobered. "In Nzadi, my job was to guard a woman who only wanted to shop her way around the world. At first I thought she was nothing more than a typical rich man's trophy wife. Blonde, beautiful, with a perfect body maintained by yearly visits to a plastic surgeon."

"But she wasn't the typical trophy wife?"

"Oh, she was, but I was wrong for judging her. She was nice enough but her life was focused on trying to make her husband happy. Like my mother did with my father. It didn't work for her, either."

"And that isn't enough for you, even now that you've seen the world, fulfilled that dream and found it lacking?" He stopped at a red light and looked toward Cara.

"Would it be for you if the roles were reversed?"

"No. What I do is in my blood. It's everything I am." Through his work he could make the world just a little safer.

"I began to feel sorry for my client. Actually became emotionally invested in her as I escorted her around Nzadi. The day we stopped at a café to get something to drink, she'd just been shopping for some children she'd met at an orphanage and had the driver take the goods back to the car. I told her we should leave. The café was crowded, not an easy place to protect her…" Cara's voice faded into silence.

"That makes sense," Connor said to keep her talking about what was bothering her.

"My client saw Obioma Dia, a woman revered by the people of Nzadi for her humanitarian causes. Obioma had been at the orphanage where my client got the idea to buy items for the children and we'd talked with her for a while. My client insisted we rest and talk with Obioma before going back out to do some more shopping for the kids. I had opened her eyes to something when I suggested we visit the orphanage the day before. I was excited about what she wanted to do so I reluctantly agreed, especially because I was impressed with what Obioma was doing in her country to help her people." Cara swallowed hard and averted her face, staring out the side window.

Connor wanted to console her. He'd heard the catch in her voice and wished he hadn't asked about Nzadi.

"That day in the café didn't go well. Someone tried to kill my client, and I prevented it by pushing her out of the way. But the bullet intended for her struck Obioma. I couldn't react fast enough to help her, too. She died in the café. I wanted to stay and help, but I had to get my client out of there. That wasn't an easy task. Some of the crowd stopped us, angry, shouting at us. Blaming us for what happened. The police came and rescued us."

"Do you blame yourself for that woman's death?"

"If I had insisted we leave earlier, when I realized it wasn't safe, she might be alive today, so yes, I do. I wanted to talk with Obioma as much as my client did."

"Did you pull the trigger that killed her?"

Cara released a slow breath out between pursed lips. "No, but our presence put the woman in jeopardy. I can't keep thinking I could have saved both of them somehow. Maybe if I had been totally focused on my job and not pulled into what Obioma was saying."

"You can't control everything, and it certainly is hard to control another person when they want to do something." He remembered back to when he had wished he could control Cara and make her stay in Clear Branch and marry him. He now realized if he had somehow managed to talk her into staying, a tragedy of a different kind would have occurred. She would have resented him in the long run. "You can't be responsible for another's actions, only your own." Constantly checking the rearview mirror, Connor pressed the accelerator as they left the outskirts of Silver Creek.

"The woman who died worked hard to make the people's lives better. There were riots in the street. Her murder touched off some unrest that had been brewing for a long time in Nzadi. The president of the country ordered the businessman, his wife and me to leave the country immediately. My client left all the gifts for the orphanage behind in her hotel room. She didn't care if they went to the children or not. She was furious at how she had been treated."

"So the children never got what they needed?"

"I told the hotel desk clerk as we were leaving about the gifts and who they were for. I can only hope someone delivered them to the orphanage, but with all the confusion and mobs, I have my doubts."

"You blame yourself for that, too?"

She shifted completely around to face him. "In my head I know it's not my fault if the necessities weren't delivered to the orphanage, but in my heart I feel as though I'm the reason if they weren't."

Pulling onto the street where Cara grew up, Connor shook his head. "The burden must be mighty heavy. Carrying around all that guilt can wear a person down. You were always realistic, so what's the real reason behind you beating yourself up over something you couldn't change? You weren't the gunman who ambushed you all in the café. You weren't given a choice about staying in the country so you could get the provisions to the children." Connor parked in her driveway and angled toward her. "What's *really* going on, Cara?"

SIX

"What do you want me to tell you?" Cara asked, trying to stall for time. She didn't know how to answer Connor's question.

"The truth."

"I've always told you the truth."

"The woman I used to know would be sad for that lady's death, but she wouldn't blame herself. She wouldn't play the 'what if' game. What if we hadn't gone to the café? What if I had dragged my client away? What if—"

"Stop it!" Anger welled up in her and spewed from her mouth as she continued, "Do you really want to know what's going on? Right before going on assignment to Nzadi, I'd been camped out in Dad's room at the hospital before he was moved to Sunny Meadows, or at least I was for a time until he made it clear he didn't want me there. I shouldn't have taken that assignment. I wasn't at my best."

"When are you going to let the past go? When are you going to quit letting your father rule your life?"

Tears flooded her eyes. She looked away, not wanting Connor to see them because there was more to the story and he would be perceptive enough to know that. The trophy wife reminded Cara a lot of her mother. The more she had been around the woman the more she saw her mom, trying to please a man who didn't have time for her. At times she'd seen the same desperation in her client's eyes as she had in her mother's.

He reached over and drew her head around until his gaze roped hers. He started to say something.

She yanked back, away from his touch. "You grew up in a loving home. I didn't. Half the time my mother was an alcoholic basket case, and the other half I was so busy trying to please my dad, I forgot how to please myself. Your childhood was perfect while let's just say mine wasn't worth repeating."

"Perfect? My father died when I was twelve."

"But you had your grandfather and mother. They were there for you all the time. I would have given anything to have someone like Mike in my life." Without waiting for him, she shoved open the door and quickly got out. "I see the contractor is here," she mumbled as she hurried toward the front porch.

The whole way across the yard she swiped at the tears rolling down her cheeks. In the past she'd always been able to shut a lid on these kinds of emotions. Why not now? Especially in front of Connor?

The sound of Connor's door slamming carried to her on the porch. She kept her back to him while she composed herself. When she swept around to greet the contractor, she pasted a smile on her mouth, needing to get this house put back together as quickly as possible. Once she did that and the assailant was found, she could get her father settled in his home, then she could leave with a clear conscious. She would have done her duty as a daughter. No regrets.

But she realized she had *a lot* of regrets. Glancing at Connor, she wished things had been different between them. She wished she had been a different person thirteen years ago.

* * *

Later that evening in Connor's grandfather's kitchen, Mike held up the pot on the stove. "Coffee, anyone?"

"I'm good, Gramps."

"Me, too." Cara nursed her caffeine-free iced tea.

Sean lifted his mug. "Not me. Fill it up. This may be another long night." After his cup was refilled, he returned his attention to the papers in front of him. "So, where do we stand now?"

Mike shuffled back to the table and sat between Connor and Cara. "I checked out that list of people you helped put in prison. Your boss lady was right. Tom Phillips is the only one out of prison, and from what I've been able to gather on him, he has been in a small town on the border of Oklahoma and Texas. I made a few calls and discovered he hasn't taken any trips lately. He's shown up for work every day. I think we can rule him out. I can't see him even paying someone to do you in. He's barely making ends meet."

"From what Kyra said, the three men don't appear to be involved in what's happening here." Talking with her employer earlier only reinforced her need to decide what she was going to do about her job. Did she want to be responsible for another human being anymore? The satisfaction of a job well done battled with the incident in Nzadi.

"Anyone else who could be after you?" Connor asked in his professional voice.

Ever since their conversation that morning in her driveway, their relationship had been purely a business one, as though they had never dated and loved each other. While her practical side applauded that, deep down she wasn't thrilled. "Not that I can come up with."

"No one in Nzadi?"

The question surprised her. She gritted her teeth and glared at Connor.

Mike perked up, glancing between Connor and her. "Nzadi? Wasn't that the country that barely avoided a revolution lately? You were there? When?"

"Two weeks ago."

"I understand Americans and other foreigners were asked to leave." Mike took a sip of his coffee.

"Yes, we were. I don't think anyone from Nzadi is involved. It's a poor country, barely hanging on right now." She narrowed her eyes to needle points, hoping Connor got the message. She didn't want to talk about it.

"It needs to be checked out, Cara. I know you don't want to discuss it, but there were some people in that country who were very angry with you whether they had a right to be or not."

She pushed to her feet, her hands gripping the table's edge as she bent forward. "The people I saw were nameless—just part of a crowd at the café and later as we traveled to the airport." She spun around and marched to the refrigerator to top off her iced tea—anything to get away from Connor for a few minutes.

"How about the president of Nzadi? He's had a hard time bringing his people under control since that incident at the café, and from what I understand, he isn't poor."

When Cara pivoted, clutching her cold glass that did nothing to cool her temper, she noticed Sean and Mike looking at her as though they were eavesdropping on a conversation that they'd accidentally stumbled into. "No, he's occupied at the moment. Besides, as you mentioned earlier, I wasn't the one who pulled the trigger. I imagine he's trying to find that person." She covered the space to the table and slid into her chair again. "Mike, did you check into Dad's stories for the past year? Any that send up red flags?"

Connor's grandfather shoved a stack of papers toward her. "I printed these. They're the big stories your dad was involved in. The last one was about the Black Serpent Gang. The one before that a federal judge. Rumor has it right before his stroke your dad was working on a piece about an interstate trucking firm. Read all of them and see what y'all think."

"This will be my bedtime reading." Cara tapped the top of the one-inch thick pile.

"Gramps, what have you come up with concerning the employees of King Construction?" Connor asked, taking part of the papers from the stack.

"I haven't found any ties with Cara or her dad. As you can see, I've listed the stories he's done in the past few years, and there isn't a connection to King Construction. There was a series of articles ten years ago concerning the construction industry and some irregularities. He targeted several big firms in the state and Washington, D.C., area, but no one who works for King Construction was involved—that I can find."

"Keep digging, Gramps. That's where the pipe and blasting powder came from. I suppose it could be someone off the street, but I have a feeling there's a link between someone at the company and the person who sent the bomb. I have my partner in Richmond looking into any criminal backgrounds of the employees."

"You don't think the actual person who made the bomb works for King Construction?" Sean asked.

Connor shook his head. "Probably not. Everyone has an alibi for the night that Cara was attacked except the receptionist who was home alone, but we know it wasn't a woman. And there was another guy, but he doesn't fit the physical description of Cara's attacker. Sean, did you find out who delivered the last package right before the bomb went off?"

Sean lifted his mug to his mouth. "None of the delivery services have a record of the package. Cara, are you sure you don't remember what the man looked like?"

"Other than the vague description I gave you, no. His ball cap was pulled down low and he had on sunglasses. No beard, but that can be changed if you want to disguise yourself. If it was the man, I can't see him delivering the package himself without disguising himself."

Connor chuckled. "Thankfully, not all criminals are smart. And your description of the deliveryman fits the one who attacked you. The same medium build—about Cara's height, one hundred sixty or seventy pounds, blond hair."

"That fits a lot of men." Cara relaxed her tensed muscles.

"I do have one other company to check out that comes from Winchester occasionally. I'll contact them tomorrow." Sean downed the rest of his coffee.

"So where does this leave us?" Cara lounged back in the hard latticed chair, trying not to show her disappointment in the lack of leads.

But she must have because Mike covered her hand with his. "We're gonna catch this guy. We aren't gonna let anything happen to you or your father. What did Doc say about your dad when you went back this afternoon?"

"The tests didn't tell him what he didn't already know. Dad's liver has been damaged. He continues to be sick to his stomach. Doc is ordering more tests to be done tomorrow. If nothing shows up, he's calling in a friend to consult with him. He might have to move him back to the hospital in Silver Creek." Her father was still upset and the sight of her seemed to trigger his temper even more than if she wasn't there. "I've asked the nurses to keep me informed if he gets worse or better." To have to watch from afar, not to be able to offer comfort to her dad hurt. As usual, he wanted to fight his battles alone.

"I'll pray for him tonight." Mike squeezed her hand, then rose. "I'm going to hit the sack. I want to start fresh tomorrow morning on the computer. I've got a feeling something is gonna happen soon."

So did she, but was it the assailant making another move or them discovering who was behind the bombing? "Good night, Mike. Thanks for all you're doing."

At the door he cocked a smile at her. "Anything for you." Then he gave her a wink and left the kitchen.

"That's my cue to leave, too." Sean took his mug to the sink. "I can find my own way out. Talk to you two tomorrow after I check with the delivery company in Winchester."

Connor followed the sheriff to the door to lock up. When he returned, Cara stared down at her glass of tea. "What do we do next? We've hit dead ends."

"Not totally. At the moment it's looking like your father may be the primary target, but we can't rule you out completely. If it is your father, then why did the man come to your hotel room and attack you?"

"I've thought about that. Maybe he thinks I know something. Maybe he was the one who delivered the package and he thinks I can ID him now."

"That could be it. If that is the case, anything you can remember about the guy will be a big help."

She massaged her fingertips into her forehead. "I'm trying. I wasn't in bodyguard mode that day."

Rising, he took her glass and his cup to the sink. "Don't force it. It'll come. Probably when you've gotten some rest."

He came back to her and offered her his hand. "Come on. We both could use a good night's sleep. Tomorrow might be a better day. Maybe I'll get the DNA results back on the blood we found and we can find a match in the database. I've been pressuring the lab about this one."

"I'd feel more optimistic if it was a fingerprint, but the man wore gloves."

"I know it's a long shot, but it will help convict him when we do find him." He drew her up. Instead of moving away, he stepped closer and slipped his hands through her short hair to cradle her head. "Tonight, you're safe. I won't let anyone hurt you in Gramps's home. Sleep knowing that."

The fierce, protective ring to his words flowed through her, fanning over every inch of her as though he cherished her. Memories of how they had once been rushed into her mind, tangling with that feeling. The sight of his lips so close ignited all those buried emotions she'd had as a teenager. She could fall in love with him so easily. Not a good time. She was too vulnerable.

But she didn't care. She was too tired to fight her feelings for Connor right now. At one time he had loved her unconditionally. What a heady thought to someone who had always felt there were conditions attached to any love shown to her by her parents.

She lifted her arms and encircled his neck, hauling him toward her. His mouth settled over hers, whisking away all doubts. For this moment she was his again. She savored the taste of him, the hint of peppermint toothpaste and coffee. He embraced her, crushing her against him as he deepened the kiss, claiming a part of her that she'd only given to him—her heart.

"Connor" slipped from her mouth, a raw utterance laced with the loneliness her life had become.

He pulled back, his gaze latching on to hers. Then it slowly traveled to her mouth and stayed there for a long moment. Finally he blinked, shook his head and stepped away, his arms falling to his sides.

"What are we doing?" Bemusement laced each of his words.

"The last time I checked we were kissing." And he was as good as he ever was.

He pivoted away. "Not smart. We've been through all that once and it didn't work out. I don't make the same mistake twice."

She wasn't going to let him ruin what they had just shared. "Just because it didn't in the past doesn't mean it can't now." The declaration rushed from her lips as though her heart had overruled her mind. "I'm not the same person." Could she risk her heart with Connor? Would it be different for them this time?

"Exactly." His hands curled into fists as he panned the kitchen as if searching for an escape.

"And neither are you."

His gaze slammed back into hers. "Exactly, again. We can't pick up where we left off. Too much has happened for that to work."

"Has it?"

"Can you tell me you are ready to settle down in one place? Can you tell me you know what you want?"

"I can't," she murmured, frustrated with herself and him. "So much has been happening lately, how can I?" The admission made her realize she'd been dreaming a few minutes ago. Her experiences shouted to her that she couldn't risk her heart.

"My point. You don't know, and I do know where I'm going. I made the mistake long ago of falling in love with you when you were wrestling with the same issue. When you came to a decision, I wasn't part of it. I won't do that again." He started for the doorway. "I will protect you. I'll find out who is after you and your dad. But—" he paused in the entrance "—I won't fall in love with you again." He uncurled his hands then balled them almost immediately. "I'm rechecking the locks. Good night."

Why were they destined to know each other only during times of emotional upheaval for her? Because it was tied to Clear Branch. Maybe things would have been different if they had met somewhere else. At least this time when they parted, she wanted to part friends. With a sigh, she grabbed the stack of papers to read and made her way to her bedroom downstairs.

Lord, if You're still listening to me, please let tomorrow be a better day. Show me what to do to help Dad. How do I get through to him?

Cara stepped outside her father's room at the nursing home/rehabilitation center the next afternoon to talk to Connor, who'd trailed her there. "Look, I'm perfectly safe here at Sunny Meadows. Dad has been calmly responding to my presence for the first time since I've been here. I don't want to leave. You go question the deliveryman in Winchester. Maybe he'll be able to tell us something. At least we now know the guy who attacked me wasn't the man at my door. It might not have even been that package that had the pipe bomb in it."

"You're sure you're safe here?"

She gestured toward the deputy sitting in a chair near the door to her father's room. "Yes, I'm sure. The perpetrator isn't going to try anything with all these people around." She was ready for some time away from Connor and his silence. Although they had been together most of the morning, other than discussing the DNA results, which hadn't matched any in the system, they hadn't said much at all to each other. She needed a break, and she suspected Connor felt that way, too.

He stared at her for a moment. "I'll be back in a couple of hours."

"Take your time. I'm determined to stay put whether Dad gets upset or not. I've come to the decision he's stuck with me, and he needs to come to terms with that fact."

Connor's mouth lifted in a half grin. "He doesn't have a chance then."

When he left, swinging around at the end of the hallway to look back at her, her pulse rate reacted by accelerating. He nodded once then disappeared around the corner. It was going to take all her willpower to keep away from him. Yet she knew she should. She owed him that much. She'd hurt him once and wouldn't do it again.

Back inside her father's room, she returned to the chair near his bed. He rolled his head toward her. He didn't smile but didn't frown, either. An improvement. She would take any little bit she could get. She eyed the magazine on his bedside table. "Do you want me to continue reading the article from *Global*?"

He struggled to form a word, which came out a pretty clear "No." Reaching with his left hand, he tried to get the plastic cup of apple juice.

The urge to help him inundated her, but she remained seated, letting him do it for himself. He grasped the drink and slowly brought it to his mouth, his arm trembling. All she wanted to do was take the cup from him and lift it to his lips. That would be the worst thing she could do. When he went to replace it on the table, she held her breath, hoping he made it. Earlier he'd spilled it on the floor. Upset with himself, he'd retreated from her for over an hour. But he hadn't gotten openly angry.

With his mission completed successfully this time, her father relaxed back on the pillows. A look of satisfaction gleamed in his eyes. "Tir—ed." He labored over each sound, but his gaze brightened, pleased at what he'd said.

"I'd be tired, too. You've had a lot going on lately. Hopefully Doc will know more after the results come back on the tests taken this morning. Are you sure you don't want anything to eat?"

He shook his head, then closed his eyes. While her father slept, she flipped through the week-old magazine, scanning the pictures of the riots in Nzadi, an article she'd chosen not to read to her dad. One of the photos showed the café where the woman had been killed. The crowd held signs, some with pictures of Obioma Dia. A heaviness in her heart invaded her whole body. She'd read more about the woman and had admired her. If only she'd been able to...

"Ca—raaa," her father said, moaning, his eyes open wide.

She dropped the magazine and leaped to her feet. As he struggled to sit up, she helped him. His face pale, he threw up onto the sheet that covered him. Sweat beaded his forehead. Cara punched the call button and held her father, feeling helpless to stop whatever was making him sick.

The nurse, her friend Kathy, rushed into the room, took one look at the situation and said, "I'll take care of this. Ask at the desk for an orderly to come here."

The look her father sent her tore at the anger she'd built up toward him over the past years. The pain and suffering in his eyes humbled her. She hurried to get an orderly, then paced in front of his door as Kathy and the orderly helped her dad.

"What happened?" the deputy asked.

"Dad got sick again."

"That's a shame. I thought he was doing well, at least until recently."

"Yeah, he was. He should have been home a couple of days ago."

"I'm sorry to hear that. Hopefully Doc will find out what's going on."

What if something else besides a medication reaction was going on? If someone was after her father, could that person have gotten to him here somehow? Thoughts tumbled around in her brain. But what? Poison? *Here?* Why was she even thinking that? People reacted to medication all the time. But maybe they needed to think outside the box.

Kathy emerged from her father's room. "Nauseated again, but he's okay now. I'll let Doc Sims know. It doesn't look like the new medication is any better than the old one. Mark's cleaning your dad up. Give him a few minutes."

"If Doc Sims is here, will you tell him I need to talk to him?" She was probably wrong about her dad being poisoned, but she needed to talk to Doc about it. All possibilities should be explored.

When Kathy returned to the nurses' station, Cara leaned against the wall while she waited. A few staff members acknowledged her with a smile that she returned. Finally she decided to slowly open the door to her father's room, being quiet in case she needed to give the orderly more time to take care of her dad. He sat on the side of the bed, his legs dangling over the side while Mark helped him. Her father's gaze linked with hers and fear blazed in his eyes. He'd never had to deal with something like this. He'd always been so healthy until the stroke eight weeks ago. Her heart went out to him.

Dad, if you'll let me, I'll be here for you and help you

adjust any way I can. She wished she could tell him that, but it would probably only make him angry.

As the orderly laid her father back against the clean sheets, he began to get agitated, trying to pull away from Mark.

Cara crossed to the bed. "Thanks for your help. I can do the rest." She sent the orderly a smile to smooth over her father's actions. Her dad hated his need for help and got upset with the people who aided him.

Mark maneuvered around her to leave. The scent of the rehabilitative center mingled with the aroma of pine cleaner. She didn't envy the orderly's job. "Call me if you need any more help," he mumbled in a deep voice.

As the orderly left, Cara watched him. Dark hair, buzz cut, medium height with a bulky body and a large stomach that protruded. She wanted to take note of the people who worked with her father. When the door closed, she turned back to her dad. "Okay?"

He shook his head.

"Are you going to be sick again?"

"Noo."

"Are you in pain?"

He picked up his left hand and plopped it onto his stomach. He tried to say something, but it came out garbled. He pinched his mouth together.

"I have Doc coming to see you." She thought about telling him her suspicions about her father being poisoned, but she wanted to talk to the doctor first. Until then she didn't want her father having anything. She'd read about poisons like arsenic being used throughout history. His symptoms sounded similar to a slow poisoning. She moved to the bedside table to take the apple juice, but the pitcher was empty. Had she poured the last bit into her father's glass? She thought there had been some left.

When Sally, one of the nurse's aides in the rehabilitation unit, came to the room a few minutes later, Cara asked, "What happened to the apple juice?"

Sally shrugged. "I can get you more if you want."

"No, I don't want my father to have anything to eat or drink for a while. His stomach is upset, and he doesn't need anything."

"Doc Sims called the nurses' station. He'll see you in his office here. He's running behind and only has a few minutes."

"Fine. Where's his office?"

"I'll show you. It's down at the end of the west corridor." Sally opened the door and stood in the entry.

She leaned over and kissed her dad. His eyes grew round. She'd rarely done that since she was a child. "I'll be right back. I have something I need to talk to Doc about. I have a theory about why you're sick that I want to run by him. I'll tell you all about it after I see him."

When she left the room, she said to the deputy, "I'm going to talk to Doc Sims. Don't let anyone in there until I get back. That includes staff."

Sally ambled down the long west corridor and gestured toward a closed door with Doc's name on it, then started back the way she came. Cara knocked, then went in expecting to find the doctor waiting. But the office was empty. She started to turn around, but something hard crashed against her skull. Darkness swallowed her.

SEVEN

"Thank you for meeting with me." Connor shook the offered hand of the man who managed the delivery service in Winchester.

"Bud is coming in from his run to talk to you. He should be here soon."

"I could use any information about that package sent to C. J. Madison in Clear Branch four days ago. Do you keep any kind of records?"

"Only payment records."

Connor took the seat across the desk from the manager. "Can you tell me how the person paid for the delivery?"

The older man typed something on his keyboard. "Yes, cash."

Connor sighed.

"There wasn't a return address?" the manager asked.

"The return address was from *Global Magazine* where C. J. Madison worked, but no one from that company sent it to him. We checked and looked into the people C.J. worked with. Nothing sent up a red flag. The package along with many others was blown up. Since it was the last one to arrive and we can't figure out where it really came from, we suspect it was the one carrying a pipe bomb."

"A pipe bomb!" Color drained from the manager's face.

"Now you see why it's important we find who sent it."

"I can tell you that the person paid extra to have it delivered by a certain time."

Connor rubbed his hands together. Interesting. The bomb had been detonated remotely—not on a timer.

"You said four days ago?"

"Yes." Connor leaned forward in his chair, clasping his hands together, his elbows on his thighs. "Do you remember anything?"

"That particular package was dropped off here at our main store. I still have video feed for that day. The person is probably on the tape."

Finally they had caught a break. "Is there any way to narrow down when he came into the store?"

"From what records I have, it was first thing in the morning, which meant it went out right away on Bud's first run." When a knock sounded on the office door, the manager called out, "Come in."

A young man with blond hair and close to six feet tall, weighing around one hundred sixty pounds, entered the room. "You wanted to see me?"

"Yes, Bud. This is Connor Fitzgerald with the Criminal Investigative Division of the Virginia State Police. He has some questions for you concerning one of your deliveries to North Pine Street in Clear Branch on Monday of this week. While you two talk, I'll get the videotape for you to look at."

After the manager left, Connor indicated that Bud take a seat next to him. The man, probably no more than twenty, folded his long length into the chair and looked at him with puzzlement in his expression. Deep lines wrinkled his forehead.

"What's this about?"

"The package you took to Clear Branch. Did you see who brought it to this store for delivery?"

"No, I was in the back when the clerk came in with it. It was to be delivered right away. Something about a birthday present."

"How big?"

The deliveryman paused, squinted at a spot over Connor's shoulder and said, "About eighteen inches long and nine inches wide. Not too heavy." He indicated the size with his hands.

Connor assessed the young man's build. He was too tall and too thin to be Cara's assailant. "Which clerk was that?"

Bud tilted his head to the side. "Mindy."

"Where were you Tuesday night after nine?"

"At my girlfriend's house."

"All night?"

"Till two."

"Write down her name and contact information."

Bud's eyes widened. He quickly took a piece of paper from the desk and scribbled something on it then passed it to Connor.

Connor rose and withdrew one of his cards. "If you can think of anything pertaining to the package or the person who wanted it delivered, you can contact me here."

As Bud disappeared into the hallway, the manager returned with a tape in his hand. "It's this one." He walked to his television set and inserted the video, fast-forwarding until he came to the time stamp he wanted.

A man of about fifty walked into the store with an oblong box and paid to have it shipped by credit card. Two minutes later a woman, wearing a floppy sun hat, came in with a package that was about the size in question. The camera was obviously mounted near the door because her face was turned away while she stood at the counter. She gave the clerk cash then swung around to leave. The hat shadowed her features, only giving him a glimpse of her lower face. He bent closer to the TV as if that would help him see her better. That was when he saw the tattoo on her arm and went cold.

A throbbing pain pulsated against her skull, reminding Cara vividly of being hit from behind. She inched her eyes open. Pitch-black surrounded her. Heat encased her in a suffocating tomb. Sweat rolled off her face; her cheek was pressed against rough material. Like a carpet in the trunk of a car that smelled of rotten fish. Slowly, more sensation reached her brain. The scent of dirty clothes. The gag over her mouth. Pieces of gravel digging into her stomach. The motion of the vehicle she was trapped in. Going fast. Smooth. Probably along a highway.

Then the fact that her hands were tied behind her back with rope that chafed her wrists. She tried to move and came into contact with what felt like a duffel bag.

When she raised her arms behind her, her fists connected with the top of the trunk, only inches from her. The darkness shut in around her, igniting her fear of closed spaces. The constriction of movement sent her heart racing. More perspiration drenched her clothing.

She drew in a deep breath through her nose and still couldn't fill her lungs enough with oxygen-rich air. Stifling. Hot.

The thought shoved her toward panic—the one thing she couldn't do if she wanted to get out of this alive.

She began to focus on Connor, who would discover her gone. On his dark brown hair with a touch of curls when he let it grow out. His slate-gray eyes that showed more emotions than he probably wanted to give away. His laugh

A SERIES OF EDGE-OF-YOUR-SEAT SUSPENSE NOVELS!

GET 2 FREE BOOKS!

2 FREE BOOKS

To get your 2 free books, affix this peel-off sticker to the reply card and mail it today!

Plus, receive

TWO FREE BONUS GIFTS!

Love Inspired®

SUSPENSE

RIVETING INSPIRATIONAL ROMANCE

We'd like to send you two free books to introduce you to the Love Inspired® Suspense series. These books are worth over $10, but are yours to keep absolutely FREE! We'll even send you two wonderful surprise gifts. You can't lose!

Each of your **FRE**E books is filled wit riveting inspirati suspense featuri Christian charac facing challenges their faith...and their lives!

GET 2 FREE BOOKS!

HURRY!
Return this card today to get 2 FREE Books and 2 FREE Bonus Gifts!

▼ DETACH AND MAIL CARD TODAY! ▼

YES! Please send me the **2 FREE Love Inspired® Suspense books** and **2 FREE gifts** for which I qualify. I understand that I am under no obligation to purchase anything further, as explained on the back of this card.

PLACE FREE GIFTS SEAL HERE

About how many NEW paperback fiction books have you purchased in the past 3 months?

❏ 0-2
FDC6

❏ 3-6
FDDJ

❏ 7 or more
FDDU

❏ I prefer the regular-print edition
123/323 IDL

❏ I prefer the larger-print edition
110/310 IDL

FIRST NAME

LAST NAME

ADDRESS

APT.#

CITY

STATE/PROV.

ZIP/POSTAL CODE

(LISUS-IV-11)

that enticed her to join in on the merriment. His kiss last night that had tempted her to forget everything.

The car slowed almost to a stop then made a turn. Suddenly, the rough road jostled her against the floor of the trunk, increasing the pounding in her head. She tried to twist onto her side, but the jarring ride kept her almost completely on her stomach. With each bounce the gravel bits dug in deeper into her flesh.

Making another attempt to roll, she felt the outline of her cell in her pocket as she ended up on her side. Hope surged through her. If she could just get to it and call for help…

The car came to a stop. The sound of a door slamming shut iced her blood. Over her hammering heartbeat she heard footsteps approaching.

Connor entered King Construction's office and headed toward the receptionist's desk. Lucy glanced up, her polite smile not reaching her eyes. She averted her attention to her computer and clicked out of a program.

"What can I do for you today?" She turned her head back toward him but her gaze avoided his.

He eyed her arm, where the markings of a tattoo were barely visible at the edge of her sleeve. "I have a few questions for you."

"I don't know anything about the missing pipe and blasting powder. I can't help you."

"That's not what I want to talk to you about." He dragged out the statement, purposefully pausing to get a reaction from her.

"It isn't? But Mr. King told me about what happened and asked me about the key in his desk. I'm gone a lot and anyone can come in here and go into his office. He doesn't stay in there that much." She ended her chattering and chewed on her bottom lip.

Connor took a seat near the desk and lounged back in the chair. Then he removed a pad from his pocket and a pen. When he peered again at Lucy, she dropped her head and stared at her lap.

Another long pause before he said, "I just came from Winchester. I paid a visit to Dayton Delivery Service."

She hunched her shoulders but didn't say anything.

"It seems you dropped off a package for C. Madison the morning of August 29th. Is that right?"

"Who told you that?" She straightened and finally looked him in the eye.

"No one."

Her eyebrows scrunched together.

"I saw it for myself on a videotape from the store. Imagine my surprise when I recognized the tattoo on your arm." He flipped open his pad and perused the blank page before him as though he were consulting his notes. "How do you know C. J. Madison? Why would you send him a birthday present?"

"I don't know C. J. Madison." She yanked her sleeve down, covering the butterfly tattoo completely.

"Then why did you send him a package that day?"

"Someone asked me to because I was going to Winchester that morning for Mr. King."

"Who?"

She shrugged.

"Do you make it a habit of delivering packages for unknown people? Are you aware that it contained a bomb that went off and that you could be charged with the crime?" he asked, although he wasn't one hundred percent sure the bomb was in that package.

Color drained from her face. She brought a trembling

hand up and brushed her long hair behind her ear. "A bomb!"

He leaned forward, all pretense of casualness gone, and said in a voice full of steel, "Who asked you to take the package to the delivery service?"

"I don't—I want to call my lawyer."

"Suit yourself. But I'll get to the bottom of this. That's a promise. And I'll take you down with whoever had you send the package."

Tears glistened in her eyes. But through the wet sheen she glared at him. Her jaw set in a hard line as though she'd fortified herself.

"Before this is over I'll have delved into every part of your life."

She reached for the phone and swiveled her chair away from Connor.

Light flooded her when the trunk was thrust open. Cara blinked, the brightness hurting her eyes. The thundering in her head increased with her heartbeat.

As her gaze adjusted, the image of her attacker came into clear view. Medium height, not heavy but not thin. He wore jeans and a white T-shirt. And a black ski mask. Thoughts tumbled one after another as she stared up into the brown eyes. The last person she'd seen had been Sally, the nurse's aide, but she was petite—certainly not this man. Someone had been waiting for her in Doc's office. Behind the door.

She tried to think but the pain in her head fogged her mind. "Why are you doing this?" she mumbled through the gag around her mouth.

The man cackled. Behind the ski mask she glimpsed a smile. His eyes glinted. "Finally I'll get my revenge."

Revenge? Who was this man? The voice was unfamiliar,

but she was sure he was disguising it with a gruffness that wasn't natural. Could it be someone from Nzadi?

"Actually, this is so much better than killing you in the hotel room." Her assailant reached behind his back and drew a gun. "Poetic justice, if I say so myself."

Again his laughter bombarded Cara. Terror seized her. He was going to murder her and she would never know why. Why did he wear a ski mask if he was going to kill her? Why didn't he want her to see his face?

With her hands bound behind her back and her feet tied together, she was at his mercy—a man who obviously *had* no mercy.

Lord, help.

He stepped forward. She stiffened. Her pulse sped through her body as quickly as the fear did. Her gaze was riveted to the barrel of the gun as the seconds ticked down. He reached for her. Shrinking back as far away from his touch as possible, she prepared to do whatever she needed to foil his plans.

But instead of grabbing her and dragging her from the trunk, her attacker knocked her shoulder against the trunk floor so that she faced him. Then he lifted his weapon and pulled the trigger.

Lucy's lawyer walked into the meeting room at King Construction fifteen minutes later. Connor sat in the chair, observing the two confer. While Connor waited, he put in a call to Cara's cell phone. It rang and rang. Why didn't she pick up?

He leaned forward and flipped his notepad open to the phone number of the nurses' station at Sunny Meadows. Kathy, Cara's friend, answered.

"Is Cara still with her dad in his room?" Connor kept his voice low.

"I don't know. I've been busy with several patients. We had one go into cardiac arrest."

"Can you check for me? It's very important. I'm worried because she hasn't answered her cell."

"Sure. I want to see how her dad's doing anyway. Where can I call you back?"

He gave her his cell number and hung up.

He started to place a call to Sean to check with his deputy when Lucy's lawyer swept around and faced Connor across the room. "My client has told you everything she knows. Unless you want to arrest her, this interview is over."

"Fine. If that's the way she wants to play it." Connor faced her. "But I want to press upon you the seriousness of the crime. I will pursue gathering evidence against you and will work with the ATF on this bombing case. The feds won't let something like this go. If you cooperate now, that will go a long way in your favor. If not…" He lifted his shoulders in a shrug.

Lucy tapped her lawyer on the shoulder and the man twisted toward her. They lowered their heads and talked some more.

Connor's cell rang and he hurried to answer it. "Fitzgerald here."

"This is Kathy at Sunny Meadow. I can't find Cara. The deputy said she left with one of the nurse's aides. They were talking about seeing Doc Sims, but he's been tied up with the patient who had a heart attack."

"Can you do me a huge favor—stay with Cara's dad and have the deputy look for Cara? Something might have happened to her. I'll be right there." Connor clicked off and started for the door.

"Wait!" Lucy took several steps toward him, alarm in

her eyes. "Is someone missing? That lady who was with you yesterday?"

"Yes, and I think she's in trouble. She wouldn't have gone off without telling someone where she was going." She'd made him a promise.

"Why would she be missing? Is she involved in the case you're working on?"

Ah. Lucy is scared. Answer her questions, and she may talk. "She was nearly killed in the explosion, and then a man attacked her in her hotel room the next night."

"Someone came after her? Why?"

"Beats me. Do *you* have any idea why?" *Please, Lord, let this be something I can use to catch this guy before he kills Cara.*

Lucy bit into her lower lip and glanced back at her lawyer. "No one was supposed to get hurt but C. J. Madison."

Connor's strides ate up the distance between him and Lucy. "What do you mean?"

Lucy's lawyer frowned at Connor. "You don't have to say anything else, Lucy. Whatever you say will be used against you."

She shook her head. "I didn't agree for anyone getting hurt but that old man. He's the one who killed my boyfriend."

The blast of the gun deafened Cara's ears as a bullet slammed into her. For a few seconds she felt nothing, then an incredible pain shot out from her shoulder to encompass her body. A groan escaped her parched throat, and she turned slightly away from her attacker as though that would protect her. Her assailant's cackles, a high and hysterical noise, reverberated through her mind in waves along with the anguish.

"You ain't dead yet, but give it a while and you'll bleed out. That is, if you don't die of heatstroke first. I parked this car in the sun. I hear the temperatures are gonna be in the high nineties. Have a nice day." The man reached for the top of the trunk and brought it down with a crashing sound.

Like a coffin's lid being shut.

"He *who?*" Connor resisted the urge to grip Lucy's arms and shake her story out of her. Time was ticking down and his fear for Cara's safety was ramping up.

"John Smith." Lucy fell into the chair near her and slumped her shoulders.

"John Smith? *Really?*" Connor moved close to her, crowding her space.

She lifted tear-filled eyes to his. "Yes, my boyfriend used to talk about his dad, John Smith, all the time. He taught him how to hunt, shoot. They used to go out camping and live off the land. They wouldn't even take a tent to sleep in." Several wet tracks rolled down her cheeks. "And C. J. Madison was responsible for his death."

Lord, she was frustrating. *"Whose?"*

"Beau's. Who do you think I'm talking about? That old man might as well have shot Beau."

The lawyer laid a hand on Lucy's shoulder. "I'd advise you not to say anything else."

Connor removed his cell from the front pocket of his jeans. "So John Smith is the one who is trying to kill C. J. Madison. Why is he after Cara then?"

"I don't know and I didn't sign on for that," she said in a tight voice as she gripped the arms of the chair, her knuckles white.

Connor called the Silver Creek police chief and told him what was going on. "I need you to send someone to detain Lucy Samuels at King Construction. I won't leave until someone arrives, but it's urgent that I get to Sunny Meadows. Someone's life may be in danger."

"An officer is on the way. We'll take her into custody."

After hanging up with the police chief, Connor punched in Sean's number, glancing at the second hand circling the clock on the wall. "I need you to get to Sunny Meadow. No one has seen Cara."

"Would she have left?"

"Not willingly. I brought her there and was going to pick her up after talking with the people in Winchester. She wanted to stay with her dad."

"I'll call Nate on duty at C.J.'s room on the way. If she's at the center, I'll find her and give you a call."

When he got off the phone, Connor shifted toward Lucy and her lawyer. They were conversing in low voices again, then the older man straightened and said, "My client is declining to say another word until a deal can be reached."

Suffocating heat engulfed Cara and scorched her mouth and throat. She tried not to focus on the burning sensation in her shoulder, but it kept pulling her back, robbing her of her attention toward freeing herself.

The coppery scent of her blood assaulted her nostrils, driving all other smells away, even the lingering aroma of gunpowder and fish. A constant reminder her life was flowing from her, pooling in the mat beneath her.

The ringing of her cell pierced through the pain, momentarily focusing her attention on the sound—until she realized she couldn't get to her phone.

"Cara, you can't let him win," she imagined Connor saying to her. "Fight. Stay alive."

But she was so tired of fighting. She'd been doing it

her whole life. The edge of darkness moved closer as she surrendered to those thoughts.

On the drive to Sunny Meadows Connor called Gramps and had him search for the names of John Smith and Beau Smith, especially in connection to C. J. Madison. Then he informed his office about what was happening on the case and solicited their assistance in tracking down information, too.

When he drove into the parking lot, several patrol cars were there already. Maybe he was overreacting, but he didn't think so. He rushed into the building to find Sean in the lobby coordinating the search of the place.

"Anything?" Connor asked after the last deputy left to search for Cara. "Where do we stand?"

"We are accounting for every employee who is supposed to be on duty. The problem with that is some have already left for the day. Shift change. I've talked with Doc, who had to leave. He'd been aware Cara wanted to see him and had planned to stop by her father's room on his way out."

"Have you interviewed the nurse's aide yet?"

"That was my next thing to do. Do you want to talk with Sally?"

"Yes, then I want to see the deputy on duty and Cara's father." Connor started for the east wing. "Keep me informed."

Connor found Sally at the east wing nurse's station, hunkered over in a chair, her hands in her lap, twisting together. "Sally, I'm Connor Fitzgerald with CID." He presented his badge then sat across from the young woman.

Her eyes dark with worry, Sally said, "I was just following directions."

"Whose?"

"Doc Sims's. I answered the phone, and he said he needed to see Cara in his office."

In his office? "Are you sure it was Doc Sims on the phone?"

"I think so. He had a deep voice like the doctor. I just started working here a couple of weeks ago. I live in Silver Creek, and I'm not that familiar with Doc Sims."

"Were you the only one at the nurses' station?"

"Yes. We've been busy today."

Connor gave her his card. "If you remember anything else, please let me know."

As he rose, she glanced up at him. "I do remember that in the background, I heard the intercom here. It came through the phone as well as the speaker over there." She gestured toward one mounted on the wall across from the nurses' station.

An inside job or a visitor to Sunny Meadows? He would need to get a list of who had been visiting patients earlier. He strode toward the deputy, who stood when he spied Connor coming down the hall.

"Nate, can you tell me how Cara appeared when she left her dad's room? Upset? Worried?"

"Worried. I got the impression she was eager to talk to Doc. She told me not to let her dad eat or drink anything. Earlier he'd gotten sick again. I guess she was concerned because he couldn't keep anything down. I thought she was gonna talk to Doc about another new medication."

"Did she say that?"

"No. But like I said, she seemed very worried."

"Anyone hanging around the room?"

"No. No one was in the hall who wasn't supposed to be. There was a patient down there—" the deputy pointed across the corridor and two doors down "—who had a heart attack. Quite a few staff members were coming and going, taking care of the lady."

"You weren't concerned when Cara didn't come back?"

The young man massaged his nape. "Well, I knew the Doc had been called into that lady's room right after Cara left, so I thought it might be a while before she saw him."

Connor dreaded the next conversation he needed to have. Years ago he'd forgiven the man, at least he had thought he had until Cara had come back into his life and he saw again the effect her dad had on her.

While the sheriff scoured the building, Connor needed help figuring out Lucy's reference to C. J. Madison being responsible for killing her boyfriend. And how did that fit in to what had happened to Cara? Urgency spurred him forward. Although C.J. was sick, Connor felt like Daniel going into the lion's den.

EIGHT

Sweat drenched Cara. She sucked in a deep breath, but she couldn't seem to get enough oxygen. Time was running out on her. Even though her assailant hadn't hit an artery, she would bleed out eventually. She had to get out of the trunk. Tensing, she began working on the ropes that bound her hands. Every move she made sent spikes of pain through her, pushing the looming darkness closer. No choice. She had to get free. The bite of the twine about her wrist didn't chafe as much as before. Then she wondered if her blood from the gunshot wound was lubricating her wrists, making the ropes a little looser.

Please, Lord, help me. Anything is possible through You. I have to protect my father.

After a few minutes of twisting and pulling her hands as far apart as possible, she rested. Her shallow breaths came out in raspy pants. The heat in the trunk as well as her blood loss siphoned what energy she had mustered.

Then a thought took hold. What if she worked herself around to where she could kick at the back of the trunk? A lot of cars were accessible from the backseat into the trunk. It might work. She had to try it because what she was doing wasn't getting her very far.

Inching her way in a slow circle, her body crammed into

the tight space like sardines in a can, Cara managed to get part of the way around when a dizzy spell overcame her and she had to stop. Her wound and the heat drew unconsciousness nearer. She couldn't pass out. She might never wake up.

"Sir, I have some questions for you." Connor positioned himself next to C.J.'s bed. "I'll try to ask ones you can answer yes or no."

The older man peered behind Connor. "Ca—raa?"

"She had to leave for a while." He wasn't ready to tell her father that she might be missing. It hadn't been confirmed, although his gut told him otherwise. He wanted C.J.'s full attention. It was imperative he find out who had targeted Cara and her dad. "Do you know a John Smith?"

With his forehead scrunched, his eyebrows drawn together, C.J. stared at the foot of the bed, then swung his gaze to Connor. "No."

"How about a Beau Smith?"

"No."

"Anyone with the name of Beau, especially in the past year or so?"

Again that thoughtful expression descended on Cara's father's face. He nodded.

"Who?"

C.J. indicated the pad and pen on the bedside table next to Connor. The man scribbled on the paper then showed Connor.

Some of the letters were legible. "Jones?"

"Yes."

"How did you know him?"

His hand shaking, C.J. toiled to spell the word.

The only letters Connor could make out were the first

few: *i, n, f, o.* The rest were unreadable as if Cara's dad had run out of energy. "An informant?"

C.J. sank back on the pillow, his eyes sliding closed.

"Sir?"

When the man looked at him again, exhaustion stared at him.

"One more question. Is Beau Jones alive?"

He shook his head as he went to sleep.

Connor stared at the man a moment, debating whether to wake him or not. At least he had a name to go on. He withdrew his cell and called Gramps. "Check out a Beau Jones. I think he died recently. He was one of C.J.'s informants. Find out what happened."

"Have you found Cara yet?"

"No," Connor said as he crossed to the door and left the room. "If she's not here, then I'm running out of places to look. Call as soon as you have something. I need to know about Beau's father. His whereabouts. Anything that might help me find the man."

As he hung up, Connor couldn't dismiss the roiling in his gut as though it were telling him he was too late.

I'll rest five minutes and try again. Cara closed her eyes in the stifling trunk, so wet from her sweat that it mingled with the blood on her. As the seconds slipped away, she found herself being lured by the comfort of the dark void. She'd have peace. No more pain. No more Connor. She'd never see him again. She would never tell him she loved him and wished somehow things could have been different between them.

She wrenched her eyes open. *No, I'm not giving up.*

Two minutes later she kicked her bound feet against the back of the trunk. The thudding noise thundered through her mind like a bass drum. Each jolt to her body intensified the pain.

Again she struck the paneling with what power she had left.

Shivering now, despite the heat, she tried to lift her legs for a third time and couldn't raise them an inch. Energy gone, she panted. Her parched mouth begged for moisture. She swallowed, generating nothing but more dryness.

She had to protect her father. She had to see Connor one more time.

From some reservoir of strength she dragged her legs up and stomped against the back wall. It gave way. Light and slightly cooler air poured into the interior.

Outside Doc's office Connor surveyed the corridor. "Someone had to have seen something," he gritted out to Sean.

The sheriff shook his head. "Myself or one of my deputies has interviewed everyone here. The last person to see Cara was Sally, who led her to the office."

Connor eyed the camera that recorded what happened in the hallway. "It's someone who is familiar with this building. There wasn't anything on the video except Sally bringing Cara then leaving. Which means the person knew about the outside door into Doc's office and used it."

"It was locked. And it didn't look like it was forced. So did the person have a key somehow?"

"Maybe we need to look at the video feed from earlier in the day. Someone could have unlocked the door then." Connor started back toward the main office at the front of the building.

"The problem will be that some of the workers come in that west door for work since they park on that side of the building. The camera doesn't pick up the area around

Doc's office. We won't be able to see who actually goes into it."

"It's a start at least. We can interview each one again, especially look at employees who have been hired recently. We know it's a man. That will narrow the search down some."

"Do we have that kind of time?"

Sean's question stopped Connor in his tracks. The reality of the situation sucker punched him. He sucked in a stabilizing breath. "No, but I don't know what else to do. We have to find the man behind this." *And pray that Cara is still alive.*

Thirty minutes later Connor wrote the last name down on the paper. "That's a total of seven men who entered the building using the west door before Cara was taken. Now to talk to each of them. Let's start with the ones who were hired—"

The ringing of his cell cut off his last sentence. Connor quickly answered it. "Yes."

"Connor," a faint frayed voice said. "I'm in a wooded— area. Don't know—where. Been…shot." Cara's words faded the more she talked.

Shot?

"Leave the cell on. We'll use the GPS to locate you. Are you all right?"

Cara didn't say anything.

Panic grabbed a chokehold on Connor. He swallowed several times then said, "Cara, hang in there. I'm coming."

Five minutes later with his heart pounding, Connor hopped into his Jeep and drove toward the woods off the highway between here and Clear Branch. He knew the area but hadn't been there in years. Dense forest and dirt roads. Sean was right behind him with an ambulance coming

from Silver Creek as well as Doc Sims. He had to be prepared for anything.

He picked up his cell again and said, "Cara, are you
there?"

Still nothing.

Pain nibbled at Cara's consciousness. She needed to
open her eyes and do something. What? For a moment
she wanted to snuggle down into the darkness—except
the throb in her shoulder demanded her attention.

Easing her eyelids up, she took stock of her surroundings, noting the vinyl interior of an older car. She peered
toward the driver's seat but saw no one in it. Or the front
passenger's seat.

A breeze drifted over her from the door—a door she
now remembered opening for air that was near one hundred degrees. She welcomed the gentle caress even though
it was hot.

Then she spied the cell on the floor near her. Where she
must have dropped it after calling Connor. She'd passed out
from exhaustion and pain after working her arms around to
her front so she could dig her phone out of her pocket. She
rolled over, moaning from the shift, and tried to reach her
cell. Shivers racked her body even though the air around
her felt like the blast of a furnace. She gritted her teeth
and stretched another few inches. Her fingertips grazed
the edge of her phone.

"Cara! Are you there?"

The most beautiful voice sounded from her phone.

"I'm here, Connor. Where are you?" Her voice barely
worked. She hoped he heard.

"I'm almost to your location. Hang in there, hon."

"Poisoned," she managed to get out, trembling even
more.

"You've been poisoned?"

"No. Dad. Get him help." Shock was setting in. She prayed Connor wasn't far away.

"I don't want to hang up."

"Please." She had to save her father. Protect him if possible.

"Okay. Five minutes away."

The sudden silence gnawed at her composure. He'd come for her. It was usually the other way around. Her helping others.

In the distance the blare of sirens echoed through the forest surrounding her. She was safe. Closing her eyes, she relaxed against the backseat. Would her warning about her dad be in time to stop what was happening to him? Did her attacker go back to Sunny Meadows to finish her father off?

I can't protect him right now. Please, Lord, watch out for him.

The prayer flowed through her thoughts as though she hadn't spent the last years denying He existed. After all she'd seen, it had been hard to reconcile herself to the fact He would let such evil in the world. Whereas Connor had grown closer to Him. What she'd been doing hadn't worked. Was Connor's way better?

The sound of a motor followed by the slam of a door echoed through the woods. From what she had seen the assailant had driven this car into the forest to this small clearing. A green wall surrounded her. Would Connor see the car through the trees?

Cara struggled to sit up. Finally in an upright position, she fortified herself with several shallow gulps of hot air. Through the open door she glimpsed Connor barreling into the clearing. He was at the vehicle, leaning inside, when others burst through the trees.

She smiled at him. "It's about time."

His chuckle bathed her in warmth that had nothing to do with the hot temperature.

After spending the night at the hospital in Silver Creek, Cara was back at Mike's house the next afternoon, trying to get comfortable in a lounge chair with her feet up in the living room. A large glass of ice water sat next to her on the end table. She couldn't drink enough and had already downed what seemed like a gallon. Across from her Mike and Sean sat on the couch while Connor paced in front of the mantel.

She'd been very lucky. The Lord *had* been with her in that car. The bullet had gone clean through her shoulder.

Connor combed his hand through his hair and held up Gramps's laptop with a picture of John Smith on the screen. "Let me get this straight. You don't recognize John Smith, Beau's father."

"No, I haven't seen him around town or at Sunny Meadow." Cara took a long sip of her water, its coolness sliding down her throat. By the time she'd reached the hospital the day before, she had been dehydrated, which had been more serious than her gunshot wound. She'd lost some blood but not enough for a transfusion. Armed with antibiotics and pain medication, she had been sent home a few hours ago.

"Take another good look at him. From the pictures we've found, his build is the same as your assailant."

"Along with a lot of other men in the state of Virginia," Cara said when Connor settled the computer on her lap. She stared at the man with brown hair in a buzz cut, brown eyes and average height and frame. "He's pretty nondescript. Nothing stands out."

Sean snorted. "Yeah, the kind that fades into the background easily. I have the police in Arlington looking for him, but so far he hasn't been at his apartment. According to the neighbors, he's been gone for several weeks. Said he was taking a camping trip."

"Another reason he's the most obvious one to be behind the murder attempts," Mike said. "Besides the fact that his son, aka Beau Jones, was found a month ago in the trunk of a car, shot and left to die. The ME estimated the young man's body had been there for several weeks. Beau was involved with the Black Serpents. That gang is into drugs and hits in the Washington, D.C., area. C.J. broke the story right before his stroke. From what C.J. told you, this man was your father's informant."

Cara had read the newspaper article when it had first been printed. No matter what was between her and her dad, she usually followed his pieces. He was very good at his job. One of the best. His exposé led to the arrest of the two top members of the gang for the murder of a judge. They were in jail awaiting trial.

Connor returned the laptop to Mike. "See if you can find any other photos of him. That one is several years old. He might have changed."

"What if he was wearing a disguise? His Facebook lists one of his hobbies as acting in local theater productions." Shifting, Cara winced when she moved the wrong way and jolted her arm, bandaged and in a sling to keep it immobile. She was glad to be at Mike's. This was the only place she felt safe even though Connor had stood guard over her while at the hospital. His presence allowed her to sleep without any fear.

"That could be it. I have a friend who can change photos around to show a person with a beard, different hair, stuff like that." Sean scrubbed his hand along his jaw.

Mike peered at the sheriff. "What's his email address? We can send him these photos and see what he can come up with."

"I'll have to call him and get it from him." Sean started to retrieve his cell.

Mike rose. "Let's go into the kitchen. I want to print some of these photos, too."

"Does he have to hook the laptop up to the printer?" Cara watched the two men disappear into the hallway.

"No, he went wireless a long time ago." Connor finally settled on the coffee table across from Cara. "My grandfather isn't too subtle. I guess he sensed I wanted to talk with you alone."

"Why?" Her pulse rate kicked up a notch.

"Ever since I found you yesterday afternoon, you have to admit things have been hectic, starting with you going to the hospital in Silver Creek. You should have stayed longer than overnight."

"I'm okay. I need to be here. I was a little dehydrated, but my gunshot wound was a through and through. I bled but it didn't damage any vital organs or hit a bone. I grant you I'll be sore for a while, but it could have been a lot worse." *Sore* was too mild a word, but she didn't want to dwell on the pain, dulled by the medication she was taking.

"Yeah, you could have been trapped in the trunk and ended up like Beau Smith."

"Which is probably exactly what my assailant wanted. It has to be John Smith. He told me what he was doing was poetic justice. That would be something Beau's dad would say."

"Your man knew too much about Sunny Meadows. He couldn't have been a casual observer, especially since your father was poisoned. There wasn't any way John Smith could have done it without being very familiar with the place."

Cara checked her watch. "I expected Doc to call by now." Before she'd left the hospital, Connor had wheeled her to her father's room to see how he was. "He told me he would keep me informed of how Dad was responding to treatment for arsenic poisoning."

"We'll give him a little longer, then I'll let you bug him."

"Chicken. Remember I'm the injured one here."

Connor pushed to his feet and covered the space between them, his large frame hovering over her. "It's not something I'm going to be able to forget anytime soon." A serious expression darkened his eyes. "This just as easily could have ended badly."

His gaze trapped her much like she'd felt in the trunk. The smoldering look stripped away her defenses as he knelt next to the lounge chair. He ran his forefinger over the curve of her jawline.

The caress sent a spiraling sensation through her, luring her closer to him. She couldn't resist the enticement of his lips, so near she could brush hers over his. All thoughts of her throbbing shoulder fled as she leaned toward him.

Their gaze still bound, he whispered against her mouth, "We'll find John Smith. I'm not letting him harm you or your dad any more."

She was the one used to protecting someone, not the other way around. But listening to Connor's husky declaration cloaked her in comfort. Her emotionally and physically exhausted body needed that. He'd been by her side for the past twenty-four hours, and it had felt so right.

"At least we have something to go on." She inched nearer to his mouth, his mint-laced breath spicing the air.

He lifted his hand to cup the back of her head. Every

sense was on alert as she waited for him to end her torment. His lips feathered hers. Her stomach plummeted, and if she hadn't been seated, she would have collapsed from the weakness that flowed through her. When his mouth took full possession of hers, she knew she'd never stopped loving Connor.

At the doorbell chiming, they broke apart. When footsteps sounded in the hallway, he rose and moved quickly back to his spot at the mantel. Mike passed the living room entrance on his way to answer the door. His glance thrown toward them glinted with a knowing twinkle. The heat of a blush infused her cheeks. Probably beet-red.

From the foyer Mike greeted Doc Sims and two seconds later they came into the living room followed by Sean.

The tired lines on Doc's face mirrored how she felt. He put his black bag down by the coffee table.

He plopped onto the couch with a deep sigh. "These past couple of days I don't wish to repeat." He looked right at her. "As I imagine you don't, either."

"Not in the next hundred years or so. How's Dad responding to the treatment?"

"We caught it in time. He should be all right."

Cara thought of all the stories about people in history being poisoned with arsenic. It wasn't something you heard as much about now, however. "So how *was* Dad poisoned with the arsenic?" Was it the apple juice? The empty pitcher flashed in her mind.

A scowl slashed Doc's thick white eyebrows together. "Through his food or something he drank most likely— quite possibly the juice that tipped you off in the first place. The first reaction that kept him at Sunny Meadows could have been due to his medication but after that it was the arsenic."

"All Dad drank was water and apple juice. The past

couple of days, he ate very little because he was sick to his stomach, but he did have liquids."

"It could have been in either one or both." Doc let out a heavy sigh. "Thank the Lord you noticed that your dad's symptoms were similar to what you read about."

"When can we bring him here? I don't want him in the hospital or Sunny Meadows any longer than is absolutely necessary." A dull pain still tap-danced against her skull.

"Only trusted people are in contact with your father, but I understand why you feel that way. Since we caught this early, I've treated him and should be able to discharge him tomorrow. I'll drop in each day and check on the both of you."

"We can't bring him here now?" Cara put the legs of her lounge chair down and then scooted forward. The brief effort siphoned her energy.

"I want to make sure he'll be all right. I've put him on some medication to counter the arsenic poisoning." Doc shifted his attention to Sean. "Sheriff, we need to find this person. He may still be at Sunny Meadows. What if he harms someone else?"

"We're working on it. We think we know who's behind this. Let me show you a picture of the man and see if you recognize him." Sean went into the kitchen, brought back a photo of John Smith and gave it to Doc.

He shook his head. "But let's show this to the staff at Sunny Meadows. What about Mark, the orderly that was with your dad that day you were taken?"

"I don't think it's him. He doesn't fit the physical description of my attacker in the hotel or at Sunny Meadows."

"Still, we'll check him out. We're taking a look at all

the new male employees." Connor leaned back against the mantel, his arms folded over his chest.

"Good." Doc peered at her. "How are you doing?"

"Okay."

"Sure you are. It's okay to tell me it hurts like the dickens. When I stop in each day, I'll be checking up on you, too. You need to take it easy, at least for a few days. If you don't take care of yourself, you'll be back in the hospital." Doc shoved himself to his feet and grabbed his bag from the floor. "Now this old man is going home to a well-deserved sleep."

Cara watched Doc Sims shuffle toward the foyer with Mike. "Sunny Meadows is one of his pet projects. Someone being poisoned there has hit him hard."

Sean nodded. "I know how he feels. My great aunt is there. The place has been so good for her. I hate the idea an employee would do that. I realize your dad was targeted for revenge, but the thought of it happening chills me. All Doc has ever wanted to do was take care of people who can't take care of themselves. Give them a nice healthy environment where they are treated with dignity." Sean started for the hallway. "Don't get me started, or you'll never get the rest Doc wants you to have. I'm leaving to double-check that your father is protected, then pay Sunny Meadows another visit. I'll feel better when he's here."

"So will I." Cara rose slowly, realizing she meant every word of what she said. She needed her father safe, where she could protect him.

She was going to use the time to forge a father-daughter relationship with him if it was at all possible. Connor was right. She needed to put her past behind her. Otherwise she couldn't move forward. Connor's kiss today made her realize until she had her life in order she couldn't explore these feelings she'd thought had died years ago. And she certainly wouldn't say anything to him until she had figured everything out. She never wanted to be responsible for hurting him again.

NINE

"Sean wasn't kidding when he said Dad would have more than one guard at the hospital." Cara stepped off the elevator and headed toward the room where two Silver Creek police officers were standing outside the door.

"Your father knows a lot of important people in Washington, D.C., and Virginia. The governor wasn't too happy when he heard about him being poisoned at Sunny Meadows. In fact, there will be a state trooper posted outside my grandfather's house." Connor showed the two police officers his badge while Cara presented her driver's license. "We're here to pick up Mr. Madison. This is his daughter."

"How did the governor find out about it?" It still amazed her that her father knew people in positions of power. But then she shouldn't be surprised because one of those gifts sitting on the dining room table the day the pipe bomb went off had been from a former president of the United States.

"The press got hold of the story. This morning Sean called to tell me that John Smith's pictures have been plastered all over the news as a person of interest. If he's out there, hopefully that will help us find him."

"But remember Mike said John Smith was a character

actor who specialized in transforming himself into different roles."

Connor opened the door to her dad's hospital room. "That's why we're having an array of different photos done of our suspect in various disguises. Sean's bringing them by this evening for you and your dad to look at. Maybe one will trigger a memory of seeing this guy."

Moving through the entrance, Cara glanced back at Connor. "What if the assailant isn't John Smith?"

"The evidence is pointing to him."

Cara looked toward her father's bed. His eyes were closed so she lowered her voice. "Evidence can be manipulated and planted." A faint memory tickled the edges of her mind, taunting her.

"My, Miss Madison, you didn't used to be this cynical."

She grinned at him. "I didn't used to be a lot of things."

"Yeah, a bodyguard isn't what I saw you becoming when we dated."

"I know. I used to bury myself in research. What did you think I would become? A librarian?"

"No, my wife."

The words hung in the air between them. The expression on his face went blank. When her father cleared his throat, Cara swept around to face him. No matter how much she loved Connor now, she wouldn't let him know. She'd hurt him a lot once, leaving town without talking to him about her decision. She'd been a coward then because she'd been afraid Connor would talk her into staying. And she'd known she couldn't stay because she'd had something to prove to herself—and her dad. Sending Connor a letter had been wrong. The least he deserved was her telling him face-to-face. Sometimes loving someone wasn't enough to make a relationship work. She'd seen her mother's love for her father, and that hadn't been enough to make their marriage work.

Even her love for her daughter hadn't been enough to keep her from killing herself. Maybe if she hadn't gone to college, her mother would still be alive. *I could have prevented Mom from taking the sleeping pills.* The words plastered the guilt that was really bothering her across her thoughts. Stopping her dead in her tracks.

For a few minutes the room faded from her awareness and she was thrust back in her mind to her mother's funeral. For the first time she remembered her father slipping his arm around her shoulder, trying to comfort her in her grief. A look of sadness in his eyes captured her and appealed to her for a few moments until she remembered her mother's sobs the nights he was gone. She'd rejected his embrace and what fragile relationship they had was altered that day.

What do You want of me, Lord?

"Cara, are you all right?" Connor took hold of her hand.

His touch brought her back to the present—to the room where her father was lying in bed, a shell of the powerful person she'd grown up with. Blinking the past away, she moved forward. "Dad, I'm here to break you out of this joint. Are you ready to leave?" She forced a lightness into her voice although her heart felt heavy.

He nodded, mumbling a few words. The last one, *time,* was the only one she understood.

She started to tell him that it was the middle of the afternoon in case he was asking about the time but decided if she was wrong that would just frustrate him. She came up with a different strategy. "Have I got a surprise for you when we get back to Clear Branch! We didn't get to have a proper birthday party the other day, so we're going to have a small one this evening. We can't pass up your sixtieth birthday. It's a milestone."

Frowning, her dad grumbled something under his breath.

"Wait till you taste the German chocolate cake I made you. From scratch. Like Mom used to."

The scowl evolved into a neutral expression.

"I also got your favorite ice cream, chocolate chip cookie dough."

Her dad's expression transformed into a half smile.

"Thanks for coming, Kathy. I can't tell you how much I appreciate your kindness and help with my father at Sunny Meadows." Cara stepped to the side to let her friend into Mike's house that evening. "Seeing someone he knew was so much easier for Dad at the center."

Kathy blushed. "He's the big celebrity in town so I've got bragging rights that I took care of him. Except—" concern inched into her expression "—someone poisoned him on my watch. Have y'all figured out anything? Who would do such a thing?"

"You saw the photo of John Smith. Did you recognize him at all?"

Shaking her head, Kathy frowned. "You think he's the one who poisoned your father?"

Frustration churned in Cara's stomach. "I don't know. Maybe. I know that Connor wants to question him." *So do I.* She wanted to look in the man's eyes and see if she recognized the eyes of her assailant.

"Speaking of Connor, what's going on with you two?" Kathy waggled her eyebrows.

"Nothing," Cara answered so fast Kathy laughed.

"Sure. I've seen how y'all look at each other. I remember how it was in high school and afterward, before…"

"Yeah, before I left town. That's the key. I left him high and dry. He'd asked me to marry him and I ran."

"But that was ages ago." Kathy moved closer. "So how do you feel now? If I wasn't married, I'd sure be interested in him. He's grown up mighty fine."

"Where is that husband of yours?" Cara hoped to divert the conversation away from her and Connor.

"Home with the kids."

When the doorbell chimed again, Kathy waved Cara toward it while she made her way into the living room. Cara checked the peephole then drew the door open with a huge smile. "Glad you could come, Sean. Are those the photos from your friend?" she asked when she saw the folder he carried.

"Yep, and I don't recognize anyone from them."

"You don't? Let me see." She took the folder from the sheriff and began going through the computer-generated pictures of John Smith in different disguises. When she spied one of them with his eye color changed from green to brown, she paused, staring at the photo altered to show a man wearing a black ski mask. Her gaze trailed down to the man's mouth then back up to his gaze. She shuddered. "I couldn't swear in court that he was the man who attacked me, but with that different eye color coupled with the ski mask…" She couldn't finish her sentence. Her throat clogged with sensations from the night she was assaulted in the hotel room. Fear nibbled at her resolve not to let the man get to her. But something else also quickly followed in its wake—a sense she was missing something.

"I thought I heard you out here," Connor said as he crossed the foyer. He took one look at her and slipped the photos from her hand to examine the top one. "Is this the guy?"

"I think so. When I just see those brown eyes and the mouth, it seems like that's him."

"Good. Now if your father can ID any of these photos, that will help us maybe figure out how he was poisoned and confirm it's John Smith."

"I keep thinking we're missing something here." Cara glanced from Sean to Connor. Her concern grew. In her head a faint throbbing still persisted, competing with the more pressing ache in her shoulder.

He furrowed his brow. "What?"

Cara smoothed her short hair behind her ears, trying to grab hold of what was bothering her, especially after she went through the photo array of the center's personnel. "What if this John Smith used someone else to give my dad the poison like he did for delivering the package? He might not be the one at Sunny Meadows who did the deed. Just the one behind it."

Sean scratched his head. "So it could be a woman who put the poison in something your dad drank or ate?"

"Could be. That would change who you all are looking into. Most of the kitchen staff are women. Cleaning people, too." Excitement, much like she'd experienced when she'd been following a promising lead in a story, pulsed through her veins.

"That opens up the list we're checking." Connor handed the photos back to Sean. "The only staff members we had down who were male and hired within the past month were two orderlies, Mark and Paul. Sally saw Mark at Sunny Meadows at the time you were kidnapped and Paul hadn't been on duty that day. We're still checking into Paul's alibi."

"John Smith could have a man planted inside just as well

as a woman. Smith had money and emptied his bank account before going fishing." Sean stared down at the photo of the man in a ski mask.

"I don't know about you all, but I feel like celebrating. This may be what we needed to break this case." With the events of the past week, she desperately wanted something to take her mind off what was happening, even if it was only for a few hours. "Let's go sing 'Happy Birthday' and cut the cake."

"I'll show your dad these photos before I leave. But I think for now, you're right. All work and no play makes for a nervous breakdown." Sean started for the living room.

Cara took a step to follow the sheriff, but Connor's hand on her uninjured arm halted her progress. His touch seared through her shirt as though he'd branded her—and now she realized he had thirteen years ago. He had her love, but she wasn't for him. He deserved someone who could give him one hundred percent. She'd left part of herself back in Nzadi. Perhaps she'd never been whole from the beginning. After all, she couldn't shake the memories of her mother. She had tried to be there for her, but when she'd gone away to George Washington University, Cara had been relieved.

"Cara, what's going on?" Connor's whispered words tickled her neck.

"Tired. My shoulder is bothering me." She glanced down at the sling she still wore to keep herself from trying to use that arm.

"We haven't talked since we brought your dad home. I know you told him about coming here. Gramps and I didn't think he would be too happy about that."

When they had pulled up to Mike's house, her father had exploded in anger. "I'm sorry about Dad's behavior earlier. He'd kept insisting at the hospital he wanted to go home. I didn't realize how much."

"Do you blame the man? I don't know too many people who are so independent and proud as your dad. Now he has to have help doing a lot of things. He has trouble communicating. This from a man who was known for his ability to get his point across in his stories."

She twisted around. "You're defending him?"

"I'm trying to put myself into his shoes. See this from his point of view."

"You don't think I can?"

"It can be hard when you're too close to a situation. You two have a history."

"And you and Dad don't?" Memories of her father's icy treatment of Connor played across her mind.

Connor's eyes softened. "Yes, but not like you and your father. I suspect the emotional impact of his stroke is harder for C.J. than the physical."

"I can't believe you're defending his angry behavior." Cara whirled around and marched into the living room. Her father had acted inexcusably earlier when she wouldn't take him to his house. He wouldn't listen to her about how damaged it still was. That it would take a while to get it habitable for him to live in.

Inside the room she came to a stop, fixing her gaze on her father sitting across the room in a wheelchair, Mike next to him. He wouldn't even be in here if Mike hadn't insisted and just let him rant and rave as Mike steered the wheelchair into the living room after dinner. One stubborn man colliding with another one.

She hated this seesawing back and forth in her feelings about her father. One minute upset with him as before, the next understanding and worry pushing everything out of the way. He was her only close family.

Suddenly she found herself imagining what it would be like in a wheelchair for a man who had always been on the go before the stroke. As she watched him listening to the people around him, his expression set in a glower, she tried to put herself in her father's place—a man who had been articulate, who had made speeches before massive audiences, who had appeared on television, not being able to communicate his thoughts well enough for most people to understand. The worst, though, was having no control over his life—a man who thrived on order, everything a certain way—his way.

Lord, what do You want from me? To forgive my father's behavior toward the ones who are trying to help him? To forgive him for all those years of rejection? To forgive him for how he treated Mom? That's too much to ask.

Forcing a smile, Cara walked to the dining room table. One candle shaped as the number sixty adorned the top of the cake. She started to try picking up the platter one-handed when Connor reached around her and took it. He brought the dessert to her father and presented it to him. After she lit the candle, she began singing "Happy Birthday." Everyone joined in.

When they finished the song, Cara said, "Do you want to blow out the candle?"

Her father drilled his gaze through her and made no move except to firm his mouth in a thin line. In the past her father had always cherished birthday celebrations and hadn't even minded he was turning sixty. That was until the stroke.

Cara blew the candle out, then Connor placed the platter on the coffee table while Mike brought the knife and plates for the cake. The fact that it was hard for her to manage certain things only using one arm hammered home even more what her father was going through.

"How many want a piece?" Cara looked around the room at Connor, Mike, Sean, Doc and Kathy. They all nodded.

When her gaze returned to her father, he said, "Yes," as clear as before the stroke.

This isn't easy for him, flittered through her mind. She sent her dad a genuine smile that came from her heart.

The stern expression on his face eased, especially when he peered at the first slice of the cake she took from Mike to give to her dad. "Th—anks."

That one word swelled her throat. She swallowed over and over, determined not to cry. But her vision blurred as Mike presented her with the next piece of the German chocolate cake.

The next morning, after taking her father back to his room on the first floor to rest, Cara reseated herself at the kitchen table with Mike and Connor. "So other than Sally and a lady in the kitchen, there were no other new female employees at Sunny Meadows in the past two months."

Mike began typing on the computer. "Yep. I'm looking up the kitchen worker then I'll check into Sally's background. I should have something for you today." An excitement softened the age lines of Connor's grandfather's face.

"Thanks, Gramps. I can use all the help I can get."

She knew that Connor was also having the CID delve into the lives of the employees, but Mike came at it from the social media angle while the police were looking more into any criminal background and job references. "So, unless we're forgetting something, there were only four new employees total recently. I was hoping for more since Sunny Meadows enlarged its facility a few months back to include the rehabilitation wing. That doesn't leave us much to go on." With her elbow on the table, Cara rested her chin in her palm and released a long breath.

Connor gave her a reassuring smile. "Sean is still checking into who else besides Sally saw Mark at work when you were kidnapped. Also, Paul's alibi."

Connor's expression threatened her resolve to move on as quickly as she could. She didn't like the feelings taking hold since she'd returned home. Her life was too messed up to pursue her love for him—not with so much unfinished business. "Is there another way to look at this? Are you tracking John Smith from his last known location? Talking to his neighbors, friends, family?"

"Yes, I've got someone on that in Arlington. So far they have confirmed a connection between Beau and Lucy Samuels. When he went missing, Lucy moved to Silver Creek and took the job at King Construction."

"Do you think she took the pipe and blasting powder, made the bomb and sent it to my dad?"

"There's nothing in her past that indicates she knows how to make a bomb. Lucy said John Smith had her send a package." Connor rose and went to the stove to pour another cup of coffee.

"She could be lying." Mike grunted. "With the internet just about anyone can figure it out, so I think it's possible."

Connor turned toward his grandfather. "Then what about the man who attacked Cara?"

"She's working with someone, but that doesn't mean she wasn't the one who stole the supplies and put the pipe bomb together. Don't you agree, Cara, that she could have?"

"Yes." Cara hated to think that the young woman, no more than twenty-two with her whole life ahead of her, would be capable of that act, but Cara had lived in the real world for a long time. From her first assignment as an investigative reporter to the last job as a bodyguard, she'd seen a lot of evil. How did Connor manage to hang on to his faith? His job exposed him to the same kind of evil.

Sitting again, Connor sipped his drink. "The police in Silver Creek are trying to get her to talk, but their hands are tied. So far she has resisted any deal they have offered her."

A noise like a thud sounded from the front porch. Connor shot to his feet, drawing his gun. As he headed toward the door, Cara followed.

"Stay back," he said in a tight voice.

Cara moved into the hallway leading to the two bedrooms downstairs, glancing around as though she expected someone to jump out at her. When she noticed her dad's door open, she frowned. She remembered closing it. Heartbeat galloping, she inched toward the entrance into her father's bedroom and peeked inside. Empty!

She took several steps into it, scanning the room for her dad. She rushed into the hallway and toward the foyer. The wide-open front door revealed her father on the porch floor, his left arm around a railing, his electric wheelchair behind him, a wicker table lying on its side. Connor knelt next to her dad, who knocked his offered hand away.

"I—can," her father said.

Connor rose and motioned away the state trooper coming around the side of the house. Connor moved back to give her dad space.

Pulse still racing, she planted herself next to Connor. "Dad, what are you doing out here?"

As he struggled to his good leg, gripping the railing, her father muttered, "Ho—me."

"You can't go home." Exasperation accented every syllable she uttered.

His scowl bore into her. "Home!"

"We can't. The house has to be repaired. Let's get you back inside." Cara laid her hand on his left arm to assist him into the wheelchair.

Although he didn't pull away, he didn't budge, either. "Now—please," he said with less force.

Cara stared into his blue eyes so like hers. The shiny sheen ripped her resolve in half. Stepping closer, she enclosed him in an embrace and murmured, "We'll go this afternoon. I promise. You need to see what the house looks like."

"This isn't a good idea, Cara." Connor got the wheelchair out of the back of his Jeep and brought it around for C.J.

Before she opened the back door to help her father out, she leaned close and whispered, "I promised him. I can't go back on that. This is important to him. Knowing my dad, he'd keep trying to get to the house to see it."

Connor surveyed the yard. "Yeah, I know. But it doesn't mean I have to like it."

"We won't stay long. Give him a quick tour then back out to the car. We've both come prepared." She patted her weapon in her holster at her waist. "And we didn't tell anyone about this unexpected outing."

"What if your assailant is watching Gramps's house?"

"You didn't see anyone on the way over here, and it's not like Clear Branch has so much traffic a car can blend into the mass of them on the road."

Connor chuckled. "Point taken. I knew the owner of all five vehicles I saw on the way here. Okay, let's get this over with."

With a little grumbling, C.J. allowed Connor to assist him into the wheelchair, then her father steered toward the porch and waited for Connor to help him up the one step.

She inserted the key into the lock of the new front door. "Dad, you'll see all the damage the bomb caused, but most of the rubble has been cleaned up. The workers are starting tomorrow and the contractor thinks he can get everything back to normal in three weeks."

She was chattering, so unlike Cara, but something had changed between her and her father this morning when C.J. tried to make his own way to his house. He'd rarely seen Cara hug her dad or vice versa, but the old man had stayed in her embrace for a few minutes and when he'd finally pulled away, there was an almost mellow look in his eyes. If he hadn't seen it himself, he wouldn't have believed it.

Inside the foyer, which had received a lot of damage, Cara paused to let her father examine the area. "The bomb blew more toward this way than the kitchen, which I'm thankful for since I was in the kitchen. It could have been worse, but that last package I put on the end of the table closer to the entryway."

Her father mumbled something.

"I didn't understand. Do you want to write it down?" She dug into her purse and retrieved a notepad and pen.

C.J. shook his head, then steered toward the dining room.

While her father viewed the destruction, Cara told him about what had happened right before the bomb went off. "This room, the kitchen and foyer are the worst areas. The back part of the house only had minor damage. I'll show you." She led the way toward his office.

Cara opened the door, stepped through the entrance and came to a halt. "This isn't the way the office was the last time I was here."

He's been here, she realized taking in the books moved, drawers opened, cushions tossed on the floor.

TEN

"He's been here," Cara repeated out loud before she realized what she was saying. Her dad didn't need to get any more upset than he was. Earlier she had discovered from her dad that the safe behind her mother's portrait had been empty the first time they had checked the office when the nightmare began.

Her father's shoulders sagged as his face fell, turning pasty. He veiled his eyes but not before she saw tears pool in them. That brought her own close to the surface. She never thought of her father as being vulnerable, but he was.

"Maybe. It could be unrelated." Connor moved into the middle of the office and turned in a full circle.

Cara laid a hand on her father, hoping he wouldn't reject her attempt to comfort. "Not likely. It's just another way he wants to toy with us."

"What if he's looking for something?" Connor waved his arm in a wide sweep, encompassing the whole room. "That's what this mess looks like."

"If it's John Smith, what would he be looking for?" Cara glanced at her father. "Is there anything he'd want?"

Dad lifted his hand and pinched the bridge of his nose,

then slowly shook his head, blinking back the tears that threatened.

"What if we're looking at this all wrong and it isn't John Smith?" Cara gave her father's shoulder a gentle squeeze.

"The evidence is pointing toward John Smith," Connor said. "He has a motive. No one has seen him in weeks in Arlington. When we find him, we'll ask him why he did this, for revenge or was he looking for something."

Flashes of the night when her assailant had her pinned to the bed flicked in and out of her mind, only to be replaced with the moment she was in the car trunk and the man had pulled the trigger and shot her. The look of hate in those dark eyes. The tense set of his body as he'd raised his arm and she'd looked straight into the barrel of the gun. But he'd worn a ski mask. *Why,* if he thought she would die?

"Cara." Wincing, her father pulled forward.

That was when she realized she gripped him like a pit bull latching onto its prey. She released the lock of her fingers and took a step back. "I'm sorry, Dad."

"Let's get out of here." Connor went through the doorway first, checking right and left.

Her father followed him. As they disappeared into the hallway, Cara swung around, her gaze skimming over the disarray—drawers emptied, books from the shelves thrown on the floor, cushions on the sofa sliced open and their insides spilling out, items on the table swept off, lying in shattered pieces. The room screamed with rage.

The rage of a father who had lost his son? The more she examined the mess, the more she reassessed her earlier comment. This was the work of someone like John Smith. The reason—the pure rage of a grieving parent.

Would her dad even have that kind of emotion where

she was concerned? Was he even capable of that kind of intensity in his feelings? She'd seen little of that over the years and only glimpses of a passionate nature, all con-nected to a story he felt driven to write. Once he'd told her he would make a difference in the world. He would make people see the evil that existed and do something about it.

But when she thought back to it, she hadn't received much from her mother, either. She could remember coming home from school and finding her passed out on her bed or crying because her father was gone yet again on a busi-ness trip. She'd wanted her mother to turn to her; she'd turned instead to a bottle of alcohol. Had her mom's drink-ing driven her father away? She'd never thought of it that way.

She shook away the memories and hurried from the office. She needed to get away from the destruction. It re-minded her too much of her life of late.

Out on the porch she locked the front door and won-dered why she bothered. But she went through the motions of securing her childhood home. Then she strode toward Connor's SUV parked in the driveway. He had finished assisting her dad into the backseat. The empty wheelchair was next to the car.

When she came around to the passenger side, Connor peered at her. "You okay?"

"I took another look at the office. It's John Smith. The person who destroyed the room was very angry. It wasn't a juvenile getting his kicks or a burglar looking to score."

"I agree."

"Then why did you say 'maybe' back there?"

"Because as a detective I have to be open to all pos-sibilities. If I make up my mind it's a certain person and only look for evidence to support that, then I may overlook something important. I can't afford to do that, especially in this case." A warmth encased her as his gaze skimmed over her features.

"Good. The person who attacked me in the hotel and left me to die in that trunk means to do deadly harm." Cara stepped closer to Connor and lowered her voice. "Not just to me but Dad, too. Until recently I always felt my father was invincible. Nothing could touch him. I was wrong. He can't protect himself now." She pointed to the wheelchair. "He can't even walk without help. What kind of man comes after a man who is down and can't defend himself?"

"It happens all the time. You've seen it. That's why there are people like us to protect them."

In that moment Cara felt a connection with Connor she'd never experienced. Before when they had dated, they had shared a love but nothing else. Their goals and dreams hadn't been similar. He'd wanted different things in life from her. And she'd been carrying around a load of guilt, she now realized. Guilt she'd taken on as a child and needed to rid herself of before she could move on.

"Connor, I'm so sorry for what happened thirteen years ago."

His forehead creased. "That's in the past. It's not important anymore."

"You believe that?"

His gaze pinned hers. "Yes. Now I suggest we leave this place." He backed up, as though he had to put a physical space between them to keep his emotional distance.

Cara opened the front passenger door while Connor twisted toward the wheelchair. The sound of a car coming down the street charged the quiet. She glanced up at the exact moment Connor slammed into her. The sound of a gunshot pierced the air. The window shattered. She went flying across the front seat with Connor following.

His body covering hers, he shouted, "Duck, C.J." Rolling off Cara, Connor drew his weapon while he assessed her. "Are you hurt?"

"No." She reached for her own gun and grabbed it as Connor slowly poked his head up over the front seat.

"The car's gone." Connor relaxed his tense muscles but still held his gun.

"All I saw was a white sedan. Did you see anything more?"

"No, only a window rolling down. I was too busy shoving you out of the way to see much more than that. Are you sure you're okay?" He scooted out the still open passenger door and placed a call to Sean.

"Fine." Pain radiated outward from her shoulder but at the moment that was the least of her worries. She lifted herself up, the intense throbbing making her careful in her movements. "Are you okay, Dad?" she asked as he struggled to a sitting position.

His gaze zoomed in on the shot-out window. Nodding, he snapped his mouth closed, a nerve in his thin face jerking.

She twisted to shut the door while Connor made his way around and stuffed the wheelchair in the back, then slipped behind the steering wheel.

He peered at her father. "We're going back to Gramps's. Sean is meeting us there."

As Connor drove toward his grandfather's, Cara stared out the gaping hole where the window had been. A jagged edge around the perimeter highlighted the danger she was in. A few inches to the left and she would have been dead. She slanted a glance at her aching shoulder. No blood leaked through the bandage. A sigh escaped her pursed lips.

"I didn't hurt you when I pushed you into the car?"

The concern in Connor's expression rendered her speechless, especially after what had just happened. She shook her head and looked straight ahead.

A fresh memory splintered her thoughts into fragments—all centered around that day in the café in Nzadi. Connor had done the same thing as she had by pushing the intended target out of the way. At least in this case no one else had been hurt. But Connor's actions had put him in harm's way. If he'd been shot because of her, she would have to live with that guilt, too.

Cara slid her gaze toward Connor. Only a few inches had made the difference between life and death. She shivered.

His look connected with hers. He reached across the space and closed his hand around hers. "This isn't your fault, either."

"Either?"

"I know what you're thinking about. Nzadi."

She started to protest but couldn't. Sinking back, she rested her head on the cushion. *Because he's right. I couldn't control what happened at the house.*

What about Nzadi? What about her mother's death?

"All I saw was white. Was it the same type of car as the one you saw a few nights ago at the hotel?" Cara said as she walked into the kitchen where Mike and Connor were sitting at the table.

"No. In fact, Sean called earlier while you were with your dad to tell me they finally found the white Ford Taurus abandoned outside of town near where you were taken. It was stolen. We checked the registration, and the owner was cleared."

She'd been sitting with her dad in his room, reading to him until he went to sleep. Today had taken a toll on him, but he was alive and now he didn't say a word about going to the house. "I guess John Smith likes the color white then. Even the car I was left in was white—reported stolen in Arlington. Are there any other white cars reported stolen in the area?"

"None yet." Connor stood and came to her. "Maybe you should go to bed, too. You look tired."

She grew taut, her good arm stiff at her side, hand curled closed. "There you go telling me what I need to do. I'm fine. What I really need is to find this guy and put an end to this terror before someone gets killed." Stepping around Connor, she moved toward the table to sit across from Mike.

"Let's list what we know and what we need to find out." Mike poised his fingers over the computer keys and looked up at them.

Connor returned to his seat. "You're really getting into this detective stuff, Gramps."

"Yup. Now I know why you like doing it. I'll go first. Main suspect is John Smith, who lives in Arlington but has been gone from his home for the past four weeks."

"Not long after my father went to Sunny Meadows." She yawned. Although she wanted to be in the middle of this conversation, she was afraid her body would demand sleep.

"A coincidence or a factor that plays into this?" Connor scooted his chair closer to the table, his expression, full of sympathy, snagging hers.

"I know coincidences happen in real life but let's say for argument sake that this isn't." The sound of Mike's typing echoed through the kitchen.

"So the person at Sunny Meadows who poisoned my father has to be someone new. Within the past four weeks."

"Not necessarily. What if John Smith paid someone to poison your dad? We don't think John is anyone at the center, even in disguise, or for that matter anyone that has visited lately. It would have been harder for a person visiting to poison your dad anyway, especially since he was being guarded."

Cara swung her full attention to Connor. "Okay. Then we really have to look at everyone who works there. At least the ones who had access to Dad on the rehabilitation unit and in the kitchen."

"I'll see if Sean can get warrants for bank records for the employees involved with your father on a daily basis. We'll start with those people first."

Another yawn escaped her mouth. Connor's gaze seized hers and held it for a long moment. Earlier she'd responded to his attempt to help her with anger. She probably should go to bed early. Her body wouldn't last long even if her mind wanted to hang in there.

"We still can't rule out new employees—Mark, Paul, Sally and that lady in the kitchen. Mark and Sally had contact with Dad on a daily basis and possibly the lady in the kitchen. Paul works in the nursing home side so he probably didn't much."

"Okay, we need Sean to first look into the records of Mark, Sally and Patricia in the kitchen. What are their backgrounds? Check their references, etcetera. I know Sunny Meadows did that already when they hired them, but they weren't looking at it the way we would." Mike finished inputting into the computer and glanced up. "I can do some tomorrow while you have your office run what I can't, Connor. Anything else?"

Connor chuckled. "I think I created a monster. Gramps, you can't do it all."

Mike squared his shoulders. "Yeah, I know law enforcement agencies have more access, but that ain't gonna stop me from trying to do what I can to help Cara."

"And I appreciate all you've done." Cara sent Mike a smile.

"Fine, Gramps. Whatever you can do is great."

"What's your next move?" Connor's grandfather relaxed back in his chair.

"I want to talk to Lucy again."

"So do I." Cara prepared herself for Connor's reaction. Lately whenever she left the house, something happened to her.

"No! Too dangerous. Besides, you need to stay here and protect your father."

"Who's going to protect me?" An imp inside her couldn't resist the question.

"I will. Who do you think taught Connor to shoot?" Mike said.

He laughed. "Gramps is better than I am. But a state trooper will be outside. I won't be gone long. I need to see if she's ready to talk after spending a few days in jail."

"No one's posted bail yet?" Cara dragged her attention from the humor in Connor's eyes. Memories of shared laughter fluttered through her, bringing a longing she shouldn't feel.

"Thankfully the judge set it high. He takes bombings seriously." Connor rose and began to pace. "I'll go tomorrow afternoon, but you have to promise me you won't leave the house for any reason."

"Hey, I didn't willingly leave Sunny Meadows."

"I know. I can't take a repeat of that."

The look Connor gave her sent her stomach plummeting. For a moment, thirteen years vanished and she felt the bond they'd had when they were young. The same connection that had scared her in the end and caused her to run.

The anniversary of her mother's death. At that time all she could think about was she wouldn't let that happen to her. She wouldn't invest that much in another to have it thrown back in her face.

"Neither can I. Child, you had me sweating that one. I never researched so much so fast. These old fingers don't cotton to typing that quickly."

The tension that had suddenly sprang up between her and Connor evaporated with Mike's words. She threw him another grin and said, "I'll try to remember that in the future."

"Okay, let's get back to this list I'm making. Maybe we should dig into Lucy's life. Find out all we can about her. Have your people in Arlington been able to discover anything about her? Maybe something you could use to crack her?"

Connor chuckled. "You've missed your calling, Gramps. Actually, the problem is they aren't finding anything out about her under the name Lucy Samuels in the Arlington area. And her prints aren't in the database."

"Where was the last place Beau lived?" Cara's mind swam with all the people involved in the case. At least now they had been able to narrow the list down some.

"Washington, D.C."

"Have they looked there?"

Connor halted his pacing and faced her. "Yes. It's a big town and nothing is checking out so far. Other than a few rumors that Beau was seeing a girl named Lucy. We don't have a photo of her."

"Maybe they should look at Beau and his life and connect her that way," Gramps said. "Why would someone admit a connection to him which gives her a motive for being part of the bombing, unless it's true?"

"That's a good question, Gramps. There must be some

thing we're not seeing. What we're doing isn't getting us anywhere, and she isn't saying anything to help us. I'll have the CID in that area look into it tomorrow."

With her elbow on the table, Cara settled her chin in her palm. "Why did she tell you she hadn't signed up to kill me, just Dad, then go quiet? Not another word after that. Even when a deal was offered."

"Another good question. One I'll ask her tomorrow."

"Could be regret." Mike began typing again while he talked. "Or she finally listened to her lawyer."

"A moment of regret that she regretted?" Connor shook his head and kneaded his neck muscles. "I don't know. There's something hard about this woman. At first glance, she seems young, not too smart, but my gut says otherwise."

Cara cocked her head. "Gramps is right. Why would she admit involvement in the first place, then not cut a deal?"

"Something has her scared." Connor retook his seat.

"Or something more powerful is motivating her." Cara's gaze trapped Connor's.

Silence ruled for several minutes until Mike closed the laptop and rose.

"I think we have a good list to start with tomorrow morning bright and early. In order for that to happen, I'm turning in. These old bones don't rally as fast as they used to." Mike shuffled toward the kitchen door. "Got to get my beauty sleep. Good night."

Cara caught a glimpse of Mike leaving, but Connor's gaze still held hers. Her heartbeat slowed to a throb. He had a knack of stripping away everything except him with just a look.

"Earlier, I wasn't trying to tell you what to do as much as trying to show you I care what happens to you. Whether you like it or not, this situation has gotten to you, especially on top of the incident in Nzadi. I worry about you." Connor leaned forward and brushed his forefingers under her eyes. "You need to take care of yourself or you won't be any good to your father."

In the past when people began planning her life and telling her what she needed to do, she'd pulled away and gone on the offense. Now she wanted to lean into his touch, draw strength from him to get through the next day. The feeling petrified her. His worry and kindness were undermining her resolve to stay away from him emotionally. Was this because of what was going on in her life, or something much more—a readiness to change her life completely?

When she tried to think of an answer to that question, her mind went blank, as though it was on overload and couldn't take on another problem to solve. The caring in his eyes pinned her to her chair even though her first urge was to bolt to her room.

"I know," she finally murmured through parched lips. "Just so you know, being here has helped with my sleeping. I think I got a good six hours last night. Better than some of the nights since coming to Clear Branch."

One corner of his mouth hitched up in a half smile while his expression gentled to something akin to how he'd looked at her when they'd dated. "I'm glad to hear that. And I realize this isn't a good time for you and me to discuss what's really happening here between us, but we'll need to when this is over. Promise me when we catch this guy you won't leave without saying goodbye this time."

"I deserved that. Believe me, I've regretted how I dealt with our relationship all those years ago. I'll be sticking around until I get Dad settled—at least a few weeks until the house is completed."

"What about your job?"

"Kyra is a wonderful employer. She understands about family and commitments. Besides, I have a lot of vacation time accumulated."

He sat back, giving her some breathing room. "Don't tell me you're one of those people who doesn't take vacations and works all the time."

"Yep. How about you?"

"Guilty. Usually the only vacations I've taken involve coming back here, and I usually end up working around the place for Gramps."

"And this time you got caught up in this case."

"Which is now a job for me. No vacation time being used. Just in case you're worried, the governor personally asked me to get to the bottom of this. According to the governor, he owes your dad. He only had good things to say about C.J.'s work."

Cara peered at the drawn shades; no light leaked through. "I know my father has done a lot of good in this world. He hates corruption and crime. All the time I grew up, he told me over and over that his life was going to count for something. He was going to leave this world a better place—one criminal at a time."

"Sorta like what I think."

"Yeah, you'd think you two would have a lot in common."

"That was the problem. We had too much in common. You." His smile became full-fledged. "Remember at that time I hadn't decided to go back to college and get my degree in criminal justice. How about you? Why did you become a reporter, then a bodyguard?"

"I'd say for the same reasons, but that's not it entirely. I became a reporter because my dad wanted me to be. And for a while it was all right. It was exciting. I was making the world a better place."

"Did it bring you closer to your father?"

His question hovered in the air between them. Cara thought back to those eight years of covering news, breaking stories—some in rough places that most people never saw. The assignments toughened her, changed her. "No. We hardly saw each other. I'd talk to him occasionally after I appeared on national TV with a story. He wanted to micromanage my life by insisting I go into 'real' journalistic reporting. He didn't want me to be a reporter for television news—only for print. I balked at that. It caused a rift between us, and then when I quit altogether, he was furious and said I was a quitter." She sighed, collapsing back against the chair. "That's when I realized I'd never please him and stopped trying. I met Kyra Morgan through an associate I'd worked with. Her female bodyguard agency intrigued me. After some extra training, I went to work for her."

"But something is wrong now?"

"I'm good at my job. I've helped a lot of people, especially women, feel safer during a difficult time in their lives, but this last assignment may be my last one." Cara yawned, covering her mouth.

"Then what do you want to do? Go back to reporting? There are probably some places you haven't seen yet."

"Always traveling can get old after a while. I still love to see new places but maybe not all the time."

"Are you leaving your job because of Nzadi? You have no reason to feel responsible for what happened there. What's really behind the guilt you've been wrestling with?"

Cara pressed her fingertips into her temples and massaged them. "You're asking some tough questions of a gal who is tired."

"You don't have to answer. I'm just interested. I sense

coming home has brought a lot of things to the surface for you."

"Some of my choices in life have hurt others. You, my mother, even that woman in Nzadi."

A shutter fell over his expression. "I'm over it. I survived." He leaned closer, intent. "But what about your mother? You never talked much about her death when you came home from college. I thought over time you would, but you didn't. You acted like you had put it behind you."

"More like buried it. I know the report said it was an accidental overdose, but I feel she committed suicide. I think she starting drinking, which she was doing more and more, and got depressed and decided to end it all by taking sleeping pills." She peered into his eyes. "I wasn't here for her when she needed someone. Dad wasn't here for her."

"So you blame yourself and your dad for her death. If it wasn't an accident, Cara, she chose to kill herself rather than get help. I know you tried to get her to go to AA, but she wouldn't. I know you spent your high school years being there for her. Sometimes we can't change others and have to accept that. Pray for them, yes. Love them, yes. Even help them as much as they will let you. But we don't have to take on their problems as our own." He reached up and brushed his hand down her jawline. "Guilt can be a good thing at times, but it can also destroy a person when not dealt with and allowed to overshadow your life."

The feel of his fingertips caressing her face nearly undid her. Her throat crammed with tears. "But maybe I could have stopped her."

"And then what if she wouldn't get help? Yes, you might have been able to prevent her death that time, but what about the next one or the one after that? Were you going to be around 24/7 guarding her from herself? Have you ever considered that your mother's problems were more than just your dad not being around? There are always two sides to an issue. Maybe when your father is better, you need to have a conversation with him about what happened when you were growing up."

She had tried as a teenager but had never found the right words. Once her mother had died, she'd stopped trying to reach him. Tears she hadn't shed since her mother's death welled to the surface and spilled down her cheeks.

Immediately Connor drew her into his embrace and held her tight against him while she let the pain from her past flow from her. The shelter of his arms calmed her as though she'd finally come home—at least for now.

When she could cry no more, she looked up at him through glistening eyes and memorized the tender expression on his face. "I realized recently I had some soul-searching to do. That it was time to stop running from my past. It was time to come to terms with my father and try to build some kind of relationship between us if possible. Only in the last day or so did I even think I had a chance to do that with him."

He cradled her face between his large hands. "It sounds like you've got some thinking to do. Let God help."

"Yes." Connor's advice felt right. She couldn't do this alone anymore. She needed help. "Thanks for listening to me."

"Anytime." He rose and pulled her to her feet. "C'mon. I'll walk you to your room before I make sure the house is locked up."

Stifling another yawn, she said, "That's okay. Go ahead and check. I think I can find my way."

He opened his mouth to say something but closed it almost immediately.

"Good night."

Cara trudged from the kitchen, barely lifting her feet from the floor.

In her room across from her dad's downstairs, she sank onto the bed and stared at the oval, multicolored rug. After talking with Connor this evening, she knew one thing. Protecting her father was her last bodyguard job. She needed to make a change in her life. But the question that plagued her was what.

Her college degree was in journalism, but as she told Connor, she didn't want to do what her dad had done. After five years of being a reporter, she'd realized that but had stayed in the business for three more years because she'd still been trying to get her father's approval. That wasn't going to happen, and slowly she was coming to accept that. She didn't need his approval. But she still wanted to figure out what she needed.

Her gaze swept around the room and lit upon the Bible sitting on the dresser. Where had that come from? It hadn't been here this morning.

Mike.

He caught her in a vulnerable mood after they had returned from her childhood home. Connor had been on the phone talking to his office and Sean. Her father had gone to his room to rest, very quiet the whole way back from his house.

Mike had found her standing at the picture window in the living room, and he'd scolded her about giving the drive-by shooter another chance at playing target practice. She'd turned toward him and blurted out her life was out of her control.

That was when he'd tilted her face up and told her to give control over to the Lord. He was a much better handler of problems than any of them.

She crossed the room and fingered the black book. She

had to do something. What she was doing wasn't working. She took the Bible back to the bed and sat. Maybe it was time to give God another chance.

ELEVEN

"**W**hat are you doing up so early?" Connor strolled across the kitchen to the coffeepot and turned it on, then glanced at the window. The slits in the blinds let in the pale light of dawn.

Cara curled her right hand around her mug of hot tea and lifted it to her lips. "I got seven solid hours of sleep. That's the best night of sleep so far."

He lounged back against the counter. "I noticed you're still wearing your sling. I thought you were going to try to do without."

She shrugged. "My shoulder was bothering me last night. I guess all that action yesterday was too much."

"You aren't invincible."

"I know that." Narrowing her eyes on him, she gritted her teeth.

"Do you? In the course of a week you've been assaulted, kidnapped, nearly blown up and shot." Frustration strengthened each of his words.

"Did you wake up on the wrong side of the bed this morning, Connor?"

He gripped the edge of the counter on each side of him. "I didn't sleep very well last night. The couch in the living room isn't that comfortable."

"Living room? What's wrong with your bed upstairs?"

"Too far away from you...r dad."

"You don't need to worry about him. I'm right across the hall from him."

Connor gestured toward her left arm in a sling. "And I see you're at your best."

Straightening, she glared at him. She pulled a small gun out of her sling and laid it on the counter. "I'll do what I need to do to protect my own father."

With a sigh, he relaxed the stiff set of his shoulders and released his grasp on the counter. "I know you will. But it's okay to accept help. You can't control everything."

"There you go again about control." Last night, as tired as she was, she had spent some time reading the Bible, praying she could learn to turn control over to the Lord. She realized she had a problem with that. She'd grown up in a household where her father controlled everything, even from a distance when he was away on an assignment. In turn she'd tried to control her mother's life and hadn't succeeded.

"I've been there. Still am. But I've learned in my job I have to depend on others to help me with an investigation."

"Where, as a bodyguard, it was all me. I had to be the one to protect the client. It's a solitary job."

"Life doesn't have to be solitary, Cara."

For the past thirteen years she'd been a loner. Actually, most of her life, except for the short time when she was with Connor. The sound of shuffling feet against the wooden floor drew her attention toward Mike entering the kitchen.

"What are you two up so early for?" He grinned and continued toward the coffeepot.

Connor poured himself a mug and one for his grand-father then handed it to him. "Just discussing the need for sleep."

"I slept like a baby and now I'm raring to go with my laptop." Mike snatched up his computer and headed toward the back door. "I'm gonna leave you two to hash out the reasons you aren't sleeping. Usually it means you're trou-bled about something."

"Yeah, I have John Smith after me. I think that's a good reason to lose a little sleep."

Mike peered back at her. "Is that all, child?"

Then before she could answer him, he disappeared out-side onto the screened-in porch.

Light poured into the kitchen when he opened the door. Every morning the sun chased away the darkness. She wished it were that easy to chase away her fears. She didn't know how to be in a relationship. She'd spent most of her life avoiding serious ones. For a short time she'd allowed herself to fall in love with Connor, but then her fears took over and she ran away.

She rose with her cup of tea. "I think I'll check to see if Dad's up."

She was running away now.

Connor watched her leave the room, standing at the sink and staring at the vacant entrance. She'd opened up last night about her mother's death. He'd always known her parents' marriage had colored her opinion of two people committing to each other. While he'd been wrestling with sleep last night, he'd come to the conclusion that if Cara couldn't put her past behind her there would be no way she could move on in a relationship with him. He'd realized he wanted that. He was falling in love with her all over again, and he was afraid in the end she would walk away as she'd done before. How could he stop himself from making the same mistake all over again?

Find John Smith and get back to his life in Richmond.

Cara let her dad struggle with buttoning his shirt until he got so frustrated he pounded the bed where he sat. Stepping forward, she started to help. He raised his arm to push her hand away.

"A friend told me recently it's okay to accept help, Dad."

He dropped his left arm back to his side, but his frown stayed in place.

"Both of your therapists are coming today to work with you. I'll mention to the OT about working on buttoning."

"Writ—ing."

"I'll tell her you really want to learn to write with your left hand. But what if I get your laptop from Sean and you use it to communicate? Is that okay?" She finished with his shirt while she talked to him.

His blue eyes brightened as though the sun had risen in them. He nodded.

"Ready to get into the wheelchair?" She brought it close to him by the bed.

His frown reappeared as he stared at the contraption that shouted to the world his inabilities.

How would she feel being in her father's shoes? Would she be frustrated, angry? Talk about lack of control in your own life. Her dad was worse than her about controlling a situation. Now he couldn't at all.

She automatically moved forward to assist him into the wheelchair. He flipped his wrist at her, shooing her away. Standing near, she was there to help if he needed it, but she allowed him to transfer himself to the wheelchair. Some function was slowly returning to his right arm and leg but it wasn't fast enough for her dad. He almost fell as he pulled up then swung his body toward the leather seat.

Inching forward, she reached toward him. He plopped into the wheelchair, peering up at her with a look of both defiance and accomplishment.

Stubborn. She shook her head. The only thing she could control here was her attitude. She had control over whether he got to her or not. Plastering a smile on her face, she walked beside him toward the door. "I can smell breakfast cooking."

Her father grunted.

"Bacon and eggs. I'm going to have to fix breakfast tomorrow morning. Something different. I have a great recipe for cinnamon rolls. What do you think?" Her father's idea of breakfast had always been a cup of black coffee and maybe a piece of toast.

A nod was her answer.

When they entered the kitchen, Mike was removing the skillet from the stove. After he scooped the scrambled eggs onto a platter, he brought it to the table. Connor came into the room behind her, his hair wet, his face shaved.

Mike said a blessing then dished some eggs onto his plate before passing it around the table. "I've run down the two orderlies—Mark and Paul's—information. Nothing in their background sends up a red flag to me, but I've printed everything out. You'd be surprised what I can discover about some people on places like Facebook. Connor, take a look at it after breakfast while I dig into the two ladies' past."

"I'm beginning to think the insider at Sunny Meadows isn't Mark or Paul. Their alibis hold up." Connor gave Cara the platter.

"I didn't think it was Mark. At least, that he wasn't my attacker." At the far end of the table for six sat the computer and a stack of printed paper. "That's all on Mark and Paul?" Cara spooned some food onto her dad's plate then hers.

"Yup. Some of it I did yesterday. Still can't find out much about Lucy Samuels. I'll let Sean and your guys see what they can come up with while I work on Sally and Patricia."

"I'll give Sean a call after breakfast." Connor dug into his breakfast. "Have one of my guys get back with his informant about her. He's the one who told us a Lucy Samuels had been involved with Beau before he went missing confirming what Lucy told us."

Cara's stomach tightened as her father labored to eat left-handed. The sight of him struggling caused tears to squeeze her throat. She swallowed several times then took a gulp of her orange juice.

"C.J., after breakfast maybe you could help me with tracking down info on Sally and Patricia. I have a feeling doing that kind of thing is old hat to you."

Her father glanced up at Mike, the left side of his mouth lifting up. "Yes."

Cara wanted to give Mike a big hug. Including her father in this investigation was just what he needed.

"They've been in the kitchen for hours working together." Cara came back into the living room where Connor had all the printed information about the orderlies spread out as well as notes he'd jotted down about the case.

"Sean's coming by to pick up these papers. I still don't see anything that implicates Mark or Paul."

"You know, one time when I came into my dad's room at Sunny Meadows, Mark was helping him and Dad was very agitated. I thought it was because the patient across the hall had died, but what if it was something else? In all of this I don't think we've really asked my dad who *he* thinks poisoned him. He's always been good at reading people. Maybe he has some insight."

"He has been in on some of our conversations about what's going on. Wouldn't he have said something then?"

"We've been talking fast. By the time he processes a reply we're on to another subject. Besides, he's still limited in how he replies. Did you ask Sean if we could have Dad's laptop back?"

"He's bringing it." Connor examined her for a long moment. "You seem calmer today about your dad."

"I'm trying to put myself in his shoes, as someone told me to do."

"Not always easy. So it's working?"

"Yes. Dad and I might not have the ideal father-daughter relationship, but I'm determined to change how I am in it. I may not be able to change him, but I can change my attitude. Because what was going on before wasn't working. He's all the family I have, and he nearly died two months ago. I'm not ready to lose him. If anything happens to him, I don't want to have any regrets."

"Good, I think—" The sound of the doorbell interrupted Connor. "That must be Sean."

"I hope he has some news. This staying around the house could get old very quickly."

Connor stood and stretched, then skirted the coffee table. When he started to pass her, he paused and took her hand. "I think you're right about not having any regrets. When my father died, I had a few. We'd argued that morning before he went to work. It was over something stupid, but I never got to tell him I was sorry." He released his grip and moved toward the front door.

Cara followed him, still stunned by what Connor had said. All those years ago she'd thought she'd known everything about him. She was discovering she hadn't. There was much more to Connor Fitzgerald than she ever realized.

Connor let Sean into the house. "I've got the info in the living room."

"The financial records we were permitted to examine haven't revealed anything unusual." The sheriff passed the laptop to Cara.

"I'll take this to Dad."

While Cara left the two men in the foyer, she heard Connor say, "Stay for lunch."

In the kitchen Cara found her father and Mike at the table, both staring at his computer, a frown on their faces. "Have you got something?"

Connor's grandfather peered up. "Maybe. There doesn't seem to be anything in Patricia's past to tie her to John Smith. She hasn't even been in Virginia long. Moved here from Oklahoma about six months ago."

"Then why the frown?" After laying her dad's laptop on the table, she slid it toward him.

"It's Sally Payne. Nothing is coming up about her. She moved here four weeks ago. Got the job at Sunny Meadows two weeks ago. I can't find anything before that. She says she came from Baltimore, but that's a bust. The only Sally Payne I could find there about her age died two months ago."

"Sally?" Cara pictured the petite woman and knew there was no way she had been her assailant—even with a ski mask on her face and her voice disguised. The physique had to be a man's. But Sally did have contact with her father. Could she be the one who poisoned him? "Let's find out if there was a Sally in John's life or Beau's. Another girlfriend maybe? John didn't have a wife. Is Sally his girlfriend? Does he have one?"

Her dad opened his computer and turned it on. "Me."

Mike grinned. "Your dad has been a big help. I'll continue my search for Sally Payne. C.J., why don't you look into women in John's or Beau's life? Maybe we can find some kind of tidbit to give the investigators in Arlington a person to interview."

Cara backed out of the room, her gaze focused on her father pecking at his keyboard with his left hand, his expression full of concentration so similar to when he'd been working on a story.

In the living room Cara sat across from Sean and Connor, who were discussing the information Mike had gathered yesterday and this morning as well as what the CID had.

Connor glanced up, a softness in his eyes. "How's it going in the kitchen?"

"Mike and Dad don't think Patricia is involved, but they're having a tough time finding Sally Payne, even in Baltimore where she said she came from. He did find a Sally Payne about the same age but she died two months ago. How did she get by the background check that Sunny Meadows would have run?"

Connor's eyebrows rose. "Good question. Let's see if any of the information on her employment application matches the dead Sally Payne."

"Like her social security number?" Sean withdrew his cell, rose and walked toward the foyer as he placed a call to the director of Sunny Meadows.

"So Sally could be connected to John Smith, too?" Cara couldn't sit another second. Tension demanded she move. She was used to being active. All this sitting around was wearing on her. She felt as though she were in a holding pattern. "The few times I've seen her, she seemed so nice and helpful. Out of the people I saw at Sunny Meadows besides Doc and Kathy, I thought she wasn't involved. She can't be more than eighteen or nineteen."

"You know as well as I do looks can be deceiving. Remember Lucy."

"Yeah, but for once I wish they weren't. Again, how do you do this day in and day out?" As a bodyguard she usually wasn't engaged in the investigation of a crime. She didn't see crime scenes except in the rare cases where she was involved in an attempt on one of her clients.

"I love a good puzzle. I'll say this one has been a challenge." As she made a trek around the room, Connor blocked her path and clasped her upper arms. "When this is over, you'll have some downtime. You came off of a difficult assignment that blew up in your face and had to jump right into this with your father."

It was more than being physically and emotionally exhausted. She was at a crossroads in her life and didn't know which way to go. *Is this where I turn it over to You, Lord?*

The feel of Connor's hands on her skin seared into her. She should step back. Keep her distance. Confusion reigned in her life and he only added to that. But she couldn't. Sighing, she inched forward and lifted her chin, her eyes meeting his.

Everything faded from her consciousness except the man before her. A man who she'd discovered would protect her with his life. He'd found her in the car and hadn't given up until she was safe. He could have been shot pushing her out of the way. He could have died for her, and she would have had to live with that knowledge.

"Promise me you'll be careful. I don't want anything like yesterday happening again. You could have been killed. I can take care of myself. You need to take care of yourself."

The gray of his eyes reflected a smoldering pool of silver. "So I should have let the person shoot you? I can't promise you that. Just like you couldn't promise someone you wouldn't do all you could to protect another. Besides, you aren't leaving this house until we find John Smith."

She'd had clients in the past who had their movements curtailed and they were often resistant. Now she knew how they felt. This whole experience gave her a different perspective of the people she'd guarded. As Connor had said, she was learning to walk in their shoes. "All I know is we'd better get to the bottom of this soon. It's hard for me to stay here cooped up, but it will be worse for my dad who already feels so confined."

Connor grinned and lifted a hand to cup her face. "You're becoming quite his champion."

While clearing his throat, Sean reentered the living room, his mouth twisted into a frown. "I asked the director to have Sally come to her office so I could talk to her. Guess what? Sally hasn't shown up for work for two days. Yesterday she called in sick, but she didn't call this morning. I have her address in Silver Creek." Sean looked toward Connor. "Hopefully she hasn't skipped town. Care to come with me to interview her?"

Eyes bound to hers, Connor slipped his hand slowly from her face, then drew back, peering at Sean. "Yeah. Let's hope she hasn't left Silver Creek." When Connor's gaze returned to hers, a smile warmed the gray depths. "You'll be all right here?"

She didn't want him to leave. What if something happened to him? Yes, he could take care of himself, but she wanted to be there, too. She couldn't be in two places at once and her father needed her more. "Of course. What more could happen to me?"

Connor's eyes widened.

"I'll be fine," she said, waving him away, a lightness in her voice. "Let me know what you find out."

He tapped the tip of her nose, laugh lines crinkling the sides of his eyes. "Will do."

As he left the house and stopped to talk to the state trooper outside, Cara couldn't shake the feeling something was going to happen soon.

Connor knocked on the garage apartment at the side of a big three-story Victorian with massive oaks shading the yard. The main house fit into the run-down neighborhood with its missing shutters and overgrown gardens that at one time might have been the showcase for the place.

"Sally left yesterday morning, and I haven't seen her since." An older woman, probably in her late seventies, came to the fence separating the two pieces of property. Behind her was a large, wooden home that needed a coat of paint.

Connor approached the lady, who was wearing a straw hat and using a cane. "Did you see her leave?"

"Yes, sirree. She was carrying a suitcase to her car. I told Ethel that her tenant had left. From the looks of her trunk, she'd packed all her belongings." The woman leaned close to Connor, one wrinkled hand gripping the top of the four-foot linked fence. "I saw her when she moved in a few weeks ago. She didn't have much then. About the same. That's why I know she skipped out on Ethel. But she didn't care. Got her money up front. It's about time Ethel got smart with her tenants." She tapped the side of her temple. "I've been educating her."

"We need to get inside. I'll go see if the owner will let us in." Sean jogged around to the front of the house.

"I imagine you know about most things that happen

around here. You're very observant." Connor gave the woman a big smile.

She laughed. "Young man, you haven't got to sweet-talk me. If she's done something wrong, I want to help. I'm not like some people that don't want to get involved. If we turn a blind eye, criminals will overrun our country."

"Did you ever talk with Sally?"

"I tried to. She wasn't very talkative. Kept to herself except for that man that came around. He stayed all night."

"I've got a picture of a man I'd like you to see." Connor pulled up his cell phone and clicked on the photo of John Smith. "Was this him?"

The petite woman dropped her cane and grasped the fence with her other hand then bent forward as much as she could while squinting at the screen. "Nope. He was young. Like Sally. I guessed her boyfriend."

"When was this?"

"Oh, let me see. The night of my favorite TV show— last Monday."

"Anything else?"

"Nope. She wasn't too friendly. I said good morning, and she just stared right through me. I don't think she liked her job."

"Why do you say that?"

"Well, I wasn't eavesdropping, mind you. I don't do that. But I did hear her and that young man talking Tuesday morning. I was watering over there." She pried her hand loose from the fence and gestured toward a hedge that would have blocked Sally's view of anyone on the other side. "Anyway she told that guy she couldn't wait until she could quit her job. She was getting tired of cleaning bedpans and listening to old people whining. I thought about squirting her with the water." She chuckled. "I didn't. That wouldn't have been neighborly."

"What kind of car did Sally drive?"

"Oh, a beauty. An old Cougar made in the mid-nineties. Red. I love red cars. When I was allowed to drive, I had one of those types of cars. Keith wouldn't let me have red. He bought a boring white one. Keith was my fourth husband."

"Did you by any chance get the license plate number?" It was a long shot but he had to ask.

"Nope. But I like sitting on my porch watching this neighborhood to make sure no hooligans take over. I'll start doing that." A twinkle sparkled in her dark eyes.

Sean came around from the front, carrying a key. "The owner didn't want to get involved, but she finally gave her permission to go into the apartment."

"Must have been your charm." Connor winked at the lady on the other side of the fence listening to every word they said.

"What's this all about, young man?"

"Attempted murder, so be careful. And if you see Sally, don't do anything. Call me." Connor handed the woman his card. "Day or night, Mrs.?"

"Flora. Wait till I tell my friends I've helped the police catch a criminal." She slipped it into the pocket on her dress and watched them as they headed for the apartment.

"I think you've got yourself a groupie. Don't be surprised if she calls you when she sees *anything* suspicious." Sean inserted the key into the lock then pushed the door open.

"I'll just have to refer her to the local police—you," Connor said with a laugh and entered the place. An air of vacancy clung to the stale, hot apartment. The air-conditioning wall unit was turned off. "Sally must be eco-friendly."

"And tidy. Nothing out of place."

Connor checked a closet in the bedroom off the living area. "You mean nothing in the place. Flora was right. She's gone and didn't bother to tell Sunny Meadows she was quitting."

"Maybe she just moved. Didn't like these digs." Sean pointed to the cockroach scurrying across the floor and disappearing under the floorboard.

"Do you have a fingerprint kit in your car?"

"Yup. I'll go get it so we can lift some prints in here hopefully."

"Yeah. The doorknob. The refrigerator handle. Since we're having a hard time finding Sally Payne maybe that will help us discover who exactly was working at Sunny Meadows."

After Sean left, Connor continued searching the apartment, careful not to leave any fingerprints. If Sally was involved in poisoning C.J., that meant John Smith had two women working for him. What about the young man Flora saw with Sally? Her boyfriend? Or another accomplice?

Sean reentered the apartment, his cell pressed to his ear, a scowl darkening his features. "Thanks. This changes everything." He clicked off and stuffed his phone back into his pocket. "This isn't good."

Tension whipped down Connor's length. "Something happen at Gramps's?"

Sean shook his head. "No, that was a park ranger. They found John Smith in a cave. Dead. Has been for several weeks."

TWELVE

"John Smith is dead?" Cara collapsed into the chair nearby in the living room. "Are the authorities sure it is him?"

"He was found several days ago and was finally identified with dental records." Connor paced in front of her, worry on his face. "They had cut off his hands, which weren't with the body, and he didn't have any identification on him. He was buried in a cave in a shallow grave. But some animals must have dug him up. Not much was left of him except his bones. A couple of guys hiking who liked to explore caves found him."

"That means we've got it all wrong then. Who's after Dad and me?"

"I don't know, but I intend to go see Lucy and get some answers. In the meantime, Sean is taking the few prints we found at Sally's apartment to the station to see if we can get a match in the system. There weren't a lot of prints. It was as if Sally had wiped it down. The ones we found might not even be hers, but it's a starting point. We need to know who is after you all."

"So, we've got two females and at least one male involved. Could it have something to do with the gang Beau was connected to?"

A frown on his face, Connor dragged his hand through his hair. "Maybe. Have Gramps and your dad begin looking into the gang members and people linked with them. I'll be back here as soon as I get through with Lucy."

"Lucy's prints weren't in the system. We need to find out everything about her."

"I know. We'll start with the gang and try to connect Lucy and Sally to it, then go from there. Remember, we can't assume anything. Look what happened concerning John Smith. We didn't challenge Lucy's brief statement about being Beau's girlfriend and helping John. We should have."

His regretful tone pushed her to her feet. She covered the distance between them and laid her hand on his arm. "We were following the leads. From what we know, Lucy at one time was Beau's girlfriend. It made sense that John Smith was behind this. Don't beat yourself up over this."

"Maybe the person we have in custody isn't the real Lucy Samuels. He shrugged away from her. "It's my job to find who is behind this. Your life is on the line. I can't afford to make a mistake."

"Hey, I can take care of myself. I'm still here despite their best efforts. You aren't the only one in this. I am involved, too."

He fisted his hands then slowly uncurled them. "I know. You can protect yourself. You don't need anyone. You've made that clear for years."

"You're twisting my words."

"Am I?" One eyebrow lifted.

"This isn't about us."

"You're fooling yourself if you don't think it is. From the beginning it has been about you and me. I told myself I should leave and let someone else find out who is targeting you and your dad, but no. I didn't listen to my common sense. I plunged right back in as if thirteen years had never happened."

"That's not true. You made it plain from the beginning you would never forget what happened back then."

"Well, guess what? I didn't listen to myself. I went right ahead even though I told myself I couldn't and fell in love with you all over again." He laughed but the sound that came out was twisted with self-loathing. "What a mistake!"

"Why?" she managed to murmur while she was still trying to digest the idea he was in love with her.

"Can you honestly tell me that you would marry me and stay in Virginia? Give up your life as a bodyguard?"

His challenge blasted her in the face, stealing her words, her thoughts. She stood there and just stared at him. The words *he loves me* kept running through her mind.

All expression wiped from his face, he peered at her with the coldness of a winter storm. "That's what I thought." Pivoting, he marched toward the foyer. "I'm going to see Lucy."

She needed to go after him, but to do what? She didn't know what she wanted. She couldn't tell him she was willing to walk away from her old life and settle down as his wife, and she wouldn't say anything until she was one hundred percent sure.

The sound of the front door slamming drove home that Connor had finally given up on her, and she couldn't blame him. He deserved so much more than what she could give him right now.

She trudged toward the kitchen to work with her dad and Mike. They had to get to the bottom of who was targeting her and her father. Their lives were on the line. But in the back of her mind, a small voice nagged her: *What kind of life do I have?*

* * *

Connor sat across from Lucy and her lawyer at the police station in Silver Creek. Her neutral expression greeted his assessment. She dropped her gaze to the table.

"Lucy isn't saying anything, Mr. Fitzgerald. This is a waste of time."

"She doesn't have to answer if she doesn't want to, but I have some information I wanted to tell her personally." He waited a few seconds. When Lucy finally reestablished eye contact, Connor continued, "John Smith's body has been discovered in a cave in the mountains not too far from here."

"Then you've got the man behind this." The lawyer started to rise.

"Not exactly. John Smith has been dead for several weeks at least, which would make it impossible for him to be behind the attempts. Dead men don't make bombs, attack people or drive by and shoot a gun." Connor lounged back in the chair. "Who are you, Lucy Samuels? It's only a matter of time before we find out. We have you connected to the bombing and possibly the murder of John Smith. Things would go so much easier if you tell me who is behind this. Because if you don't talk, you'll be charged with more serious crimes. All you have to have is knowledge of the crimes. Withholding evidence will make you just as guilty. Not to mention attempted murder of a police officer—me. You may not have been the one who shot at me in the drive-by, but you've been caught up in the conspiracy from the beginning. The charges are adding up. Longer time in jail."

She turned to her lawyer and whispered something to him.

"She has nothing to say. Now, if you'll excuse me, I have other clients I need to see."

"Lucy, we're investigating your connection to the Washington, D.C. gang, and we'll find it. If you're connected to them, we can protect you."

Her gaze flared for a couple of seconds before she managed to wipe any expression from her eyes. "I told you I was Beau's girlfriend."

"Anyone else's in the gang? Is this revenge for C. J. Madison's article that brought the leaders finally to trial?"

Lucy kept her head down. "I want to go back to my cell. I have nothing to say."

Her lawyer stood, assisting Lucy to her feet. "This interview is over."

"Suit yourself." Connor walked toward the door. "I hope you get used to living in a cell. It'll be your home until you grow old and gray." He walked out of the room and indicated to the police officer he was finished talking to Lucy.

On the drive to the station, his thoughts had constantly slipped to his conversation with Cara, and he'd struggled to stay focused on his meeting with Lucy. He'd known it was a long shot interviewing her yet again, but he'd had to try. And he'd discovered what he needed to. Lucy was linked with the gang somehow—beyond her connection to Beau.

What if Lucy is playing me again? The question plagued him as he left the building. His gut said no, but he could be wrong. On the way back to his grandfather's, he stopped by to talk with Sean.

"I found a picture of the gang leader's lieutenant's girlfriend." Mike grinned and turned the laptop toward Cara. "Do you know her?"

"That's Lucy!" Although, Lucy was dressed differently, in jeans with holes and a short-cropped shirt that emphasized parts of her body she wanted to show off. The photo revealed the same long brown hair, no longer pulled back in a ponytail, but a wild mass of curls. The clean face of the receptionist at the construction company was replaced with one that was heavily made up. The red-colored smiling lips mocked Cara as she stared at the woman next to her boyfriend, draped all over him. "When was this picture taken?"

"Right before the two gang leaders were arrested two months ago. Now all I have to do is find out this woman's name." Mike took the computer back and began typing in a command.

"It seems Lucy didn't really care about Beau like she proclaims. It didn't take her long to move on."

Cara busied herself going through the papers they had printed, trying to find a connection between Sally and Lucy, but her conversation with Connor kept intruding into her thoughts. She often had to reread a sentence. Frustration caused her to rise and walk to the sink for some more water. She stood looking out the window at the backyard. As the sun began its descent toward the western horizon, shadows began to lengthen, highlighting the openness of Mike's place—on the outskirts of town, several acres surrounding his house. Yes, his lawn out back was fenced, but the chain-link barrier could be easily scaled.

"Gooot—it."

Her father's voice pulled her attention away from her thoughts. She pivoted and saw the lopsided grin on his face. Dad leaned to the side while Mike looked at her father's computer screen.

Mike glanced up at her. "C.J. found out who Sally really is. She's Brandy Owens and she's the girlfriend of the leader of the gang. The one awaiting trial with the second in command."

"I'll call Connor and let him know. We know from the CID officer's informant there was a Lucy Samuels who dated Beau. What if our Lucy is the same one? She might have been the one to turn Beau in to the gang as an informant that led to his murder."

"We'll keep working and let you know."

Cara shifted her gaze to her father and smiled. "You haven't lost your touch, Dad. Now that we know Sally's real name, Connor and Sean might be able to find where she's gone. Also, Connor's contacts in the Washington area can find out if there is one Lucy or two different people. I feel things are starting to fall into place."

The look in her dad's eyes warmed. He nodded and went back to work.

Cara withdrew her cell from her jeans pocket and ambled toward the living room while she punched in Connor's number. Her stomach constricted as she waited for him to answer.

"I'll tell Sean, Cara. We'll be able to alert cops to be on the lookout for Sally's car with a license number to go with the description the neighbor gave." Connor sat in the sheriff's office across from Sean but made a point not to look at his friend. He was afraid something in his expression would give himself away. "I'll be back at the house soon."

When he hung up, Connor took his time putting away his cell while looking away from Sean. He wanted nothing showing on his face. The sound of Cara's excited voice still filled him with emotions he wanted to deny. How could he fall in love with her again after all his talk of not doing that? Because he'd never fallen out of love with her. That explanation hit him in the gut as though a boxer had landed a knockout blow.

"What did they find out?" Sean asked.

"Sally Payne is really Brandy Owens."

Sean turned to his computer on his desk and checked on Brandy's vehicle's license number. "Got it. I'll get this out to everyone here and let the police in Silver Creek know, too. Be right back."

While his friend was gone, Connor contacted his office and gave them the update. "I want to know everything there is to know about this gang in Washington. Who's running it while the leaders are in jail? Who can't be accounted for? Maybe some of the gang members are helping Brandy go after C.J. I want pressure put on this gang, especially the two behind bars. Bring the gang members in and make them sweat. We've helped the D.C. police before. Have them work their contacts on the street." Connor ended the call and closed his cell.

"We're especially looking around the lake," Sean said as he reentered his office. "There's a lot of rental property where someone could be holed up. I called the authorities in Winchester and a few other surrounding towns."

"Hopefully something will turn up soon." Connor rose. "I'm going home. I'll make a few more calls when I get there. I have some friends in D.C. who owe me."

"I'm heading to dinner soon then back here to work some more." As he strode toward the door, Sean grinned. "Tell Cara hi for me. I imagine being cooped up with you three in that house is driving her crazy about now."

"No, it's driving *me* crazy," Connor muttered, leaving Sean's office.

"What did you say?" Sean came up behind him.

"Nothing. Just some grumblings. Not enough sleep."

"Ah, she's getting to you. I wondered when it would happen."

Over his shoulder Connor glimpsed the smug look on

Sean's face. "Not another word if you want to remain my friend."

The sheriff's chuckles grated on Connor's nerves all the way to the front door of the station. Outside, as the sun began to set, quiet ruled, except for an occasional car passing by the sheriff's office on the road leading toward Silver Creek. He paused and breathed in deep gulps of the hot summer air. Although Gramps's place was on the other side of Clear Branch, it would only take him ten minutes to get there. Ten minutes and he would see Cara again.

Ten minutes and he would have to act as though he *wasn't* in love with her because he was bound and determined to mean it this time. Loving Cara Madison was not good for him.

Slowly he made his way to his Jeep parked at the side of the building. His thoughts centered on Cara, Connor didn't notice a man swiftly moving toward him until it was too late.

A tall, muscular man with tattoos all over him held a gun in his hand, and it was pointed at Connor.

"Got Lucy's name. It's Lucy Samuels." Mike pumped his arm into the air.

Cara stood at the stove cooking spaghetti and meat sauce. "So she used her real name. Not like Brandy Owens, aka Sally Payne."

"Yeah, surprise, surprise."

"Connor should be here soon." Cara put the wooden spoon on the counter. "Would you watch the sauce? I'm going to get Dad for dinner."

"He's been a real trooper through all this."

She stopped at the doorway. "Trooper?"

"Yeah, he's been working as hard as I have until half

an hour ago, and I haven't been poisoned and had a stroke. Have you noticed how much he's trying today?"

"Yes, but…"

"Child, I'll be the first to admit I've never been a big fan of your father on a personal level. As a professional he's top-notch. He's made a difference with his reporting."

"I'll keep that in mind." Cara quickly left the kitchen and went down the hall toward her father's bedroom where he went to lie down for a few minutes.

After a brief knock on the door she opened it and poked her head in to tell him dinner was almost ready. The room was empty.

The fact that Connor could identify the man holding the gun on him reinforced the gravity of the situation. The tattooed thug didn't intend to rob him and flee. This was tied to what was going on with Cara, and he would be a dead man if he couldn't overpower his assailant. These thoughts flew through Connor's mind as his gaze fastened onto the weapon pointed at his heart only feet from him.

"What do you want?" Connor asked, lifting his attention to the man's face, imprinting his features on his mind in case he managed to survive.

"Nothing you can give me, man." His gruff, gravelly voice cut through the hot air like a sword.

Connor calculated his chances of outrunning a bullet and came up nil. "We know about the connection to the murder attempts and the Black Serpents."

Tattoo man narrowed his eyes. "No one challenges us."

"Connor, I have news about Brandy," Sean said as he came around the corner of the building and came to a stop.

* * *

Cara's heartbeat kicked up a notch. *Where's Dad?* She backed out of his bedroom into the hall and glanced around. Then she heard a groaning sound coming from her room.

She whirled around and charged through the doorway, half expecting to see someone inside besides her dad. His eyes grew round at the sight of her rushing into the middle of the room, her gun drawn. He had been in the process of either standing or sitting again in his wheelchair. Plopping the rest of the way into the leather seat, he twisted his mouth into a frown while splaying his left hand over his heart.

Holstering her gun, Cara tried to laugh at her assumption her father was in danger and her becoming a one-woman cavalry, minus the horse. "Sorry. I thought you were in trouble. I heard your groan."

He fumbled for the pad in the pocket at the side of his wheelchair and laid it on his lap. As she made her way toward him by the window, the sheers drawn but the curtains open to let in daylight, her father jotted down a note.

She picked it up and read, "Hear noise. Check came." She looked at him and asked, "Inside here?"

He shook his head.

"Outside?"

"Yes."

"By my window?"

He shrugged, then wrote something else on the paper. *Side house.*

Cara leaned around her father and closed the curtains, shutting out the darkness descending since the sun began to set. The light from the hallway illuminated the path while he steered his wheelchair from the room.

"I don't want you near a window. Somebody could have seen you and tried to shoot you. I'll give the guard outside a call and let him check it out. That's his job. Not ours."

She said it out loud, not only to convince her father but also herself because her first instinct was to deposit her dad with Mike then go around to the side of the house and see what could have gotten her father's attention. As they headed toward the kitchen, Cara made the call to the guard, who said he would check it out.

"The state trooper said it was probably a dog he saw earlier roaming the neighborhood. He thinks he got into the garbage cans kept near the gate," she said, slipping her cell into her pocket.

When they entered the room, Mike turned off the stove and brought the pot of spaghetti to the sink to pour into the colander. "I was about to send out a search party. Dinner is almost ready. I've got to get something upstairs. Connor should be home by then and we can eat."

"I'll go on and put everything on the table, then give him a call if he isn't here by then." While her father rolled to the table, Cara headed for the cabinet to get the dishes.

"You know, Dad, it might be nice to have you come to Dallas for a while. Once the perpetrator is caught, a change of scenery might be just the thing you need. I hope you'll think about that." She set a glass on each place mat. "You hardly ever go on a vacation. We could go see some sights in Texas." As she made the offer, a part of her was in full panic that her father would accept her invitation. What would they talk about? Would they argue the whole time?

But when she saw his surprised expression, she realized it had been the right thing to do whether he accepted or not. Maybe it wasn't too late for them. Maybe they could have some kind of a father-daughter relationship. He had faced death with his stroke. That could change a person.

She sat in a chair that she turned to face her father, taking his hands in hers. "I know our past relationship has been rocky at best, but that doesn't mean our future has to be. I hope you'll slow down and take time to enjoy life. Work is important, but it isn't everything." She half expected her dad to tug his hands away but he didn't.

He stared at her for a long moment, tears slowly filling his eyes. "A—greeee."

Cara's throat closed. "You could come while the house is being finished, and then I could bring you back when the renovations are completed. That's if Doc okays it."

He nodded.

There were a lot of things she wanted to talk to her father about, but once she'd let go of her anger toward him, especially concerning her mother, answers to questions she'd had for years weren't that important anymore. She was discovering forgiving him was more for herself than anyone else. For the first time in a long while, she felt free of the past. Could she use that to make some kind of sense concerning her feelings for Connor?

"Good. We'll ask Doc when he comes to see you tomorrow." She squeezed his hands, then lounged back in the chair, cherishing the link with her father.

A faint smell wafted to her that quickly grew stronger. *Something's burning?*

She'd put rolls into the oven, but she'd thought she'd turned it off before going to look for her dad. Swiveling around, she peered at the stove but couldn't tell from this angle so she decided to get up and check to make sure.

Her father's forehead crinkled as he drew in a deep breath.

"The rolls must be burning," Cara said as she hurried to

the oven and pulled down its door. Lightly browned rolls greeted her inspection and no blast of heat rolled from the interior.

She straightened and looked around. The scent of smoke invading the kitchen was coming at her from all sides now.

THIRTEEN

Tattoo man swerved his full attention toward Sean—only seconds—but long enough that Connor lunged toward him, grabbing for the hand that held the gun. A shot erupted from the barrel, blasting the air close to his ear. A ringing sound vibrated through his head as Connor threw all his weight into taking the thug down.

Their bodies slammed into the pavement between his SUV and a police cruiser. Locked in a bear hug, the weapon between them, Connor wrestled for control of the gun. The fierce grimace on the gang member's face mirrored how Connor felt.

The sound of running footsteps nipped at the edge of his mind, but he dismissed it and totally focused on turning the barrel away from his head. Inch by inch it moved toward Tattoo man.

"Police. Drop the gun."

Connor sensed Sean hovering over them, but he didn't take his eyes off his assailant. The thug continued to grapple for the gun, but his hand shook. "Give it up. You can't escape."

The man swung his gaze to Sean then back to Connor. Dark pinpoints penetrated through him. If they had been lethal, he would have been dead.

Seconds evolved into a minute.

Sean knelt and placed the barrel at the side of the man's temple. "Don't be stupid."

As his friend said those words, Tattoo man let up a fraction, giving Connor the chance to point the gun at the gang member, right under his chin.

His attacker blinked and released his grasp on the weapon.

"First smart move you've made today," Sean said as Connor slowly rose with the gun in his hand.

"On your stomach." Sean stood, his gun on the gang member as he complied. Then Sean took his handcuffs and snapped them on the man's wrists.

Connor finally inhaled a steadying breath while he helped the suspect stand. "What were you going to tell me about Brandy?"

"One of my deputies spotted her car at a cabin on the lake." Sean directed the man toward the front of the sheriff's station.

"Was she there?"

"No, but he's checking the area out."

"I was heading out to organize a manhunt, or in this case a womanhunt."

"I can interview this guy if you need to go to the lake."

"That's what I was hoping you would say. I'll call you if anything turns up. Do you think he was Cara's assailant?"

As a deputy led the suspect inside to an interview room, Connor assessed him. "He's the right height and weight to be Cara's attacker. Once I talk with him, I might have Cara come down here to see if she can identify him."

"Guess you're gonna miss your dinner, too."

"Yeah, Cara's cooking spaghetti tonight."

"You sound downright domestic. What's going on with you two?"

"Nothing." And that was the problem. Cara was determined to go through life alone, and he needed to once and for all realize that and move on. He wanted a family. He wanted a commitment.

After Sean left the station, Connor started toward the interview room but stopped halfway there. He'd better call Gramps and let him know he wouldn't be home right away and to eat without him.

On the fifth ring, when the voice mail came on, Connor said, "Call me back. There have been some developments in the case." Not too concerned, he knew that his grandfather didn't always move fast enough to pick up before the answering machine clicked on. He usually called right back. But wouldn't Cara have heard the phone and got it?

He waited a minute for Gramps to return the call, the seconds ticking by excruciatingly slow. When he didn't, Connor tried Cara's cell. He got her voice mail. His alarm spiked. The last call he made was to the state trooper guarding Gramps's house. When he didn't get an answer, he stuffed his cell into his pocket and strode toward the exit.

"I'll interview the suspect later," Connor said to the deputy behind the counter.

As he covered the distance to his SUV, he gave Cara another call. Still no answer. Only her voice mail. He gritted his teeth and wrenched open the driver's side door. His gut roiled and all his instincts told him something was very wrong at the house.

Smoky tentacles snaked into the kitchen from the dining room and hallway. Cara hurried to her father and commandeered his wheelchair, pointing it toward the back door. "We've got to get out of here."

Her dad peered back at her. "Mike?"

"I'll get you outside then come back for him." She reached around him to open the door.

It was locked. She searched the area for the key that unlocked the deadbolt. She couldn't find it. Then she remembered Mike checking the door right after Connor left and putting the key in his pocket, as was his habit when he was home alone.

The smell of smoke grew stronger. Her father coughed. She rushed to the sink and wet a cloth for herself and her dad. After shedding her sling so she could use both hands, she tied the dishrag around his face, covering his mouth and nose. She knew where the key was kept for the front—in a bowl on the table near the exit.

"We have to go out the front." After fixing the cloth around her, her left arm protesting the strain, she guided the wheelchair toward the hallway that led to the foyer.

A thick wall of smoke obscured her path.

Then she saw them—flames consuming the front door and licking their way across the foyer and up the stairs.

Mike! *Lord, help him. Us.*

She maneuvered the wheelchair back into the kitchen and shut the door, then scanned the room for another way out. Her gaze lit upon the large window by the table. The other one was over the sink and smaller. She went to it and tugged on it. It didn't budge—because Mike had nailed all the ones on the first floor shut to make it harder for someone to get into the house.

Trapped by their security measures.

She searched the kitchen for something to use to break the glass. She found the wooden hammer used to tenderize meat and took it. As she started for the window, her father coughed again, drawing her attention. His cloth had fallen down, circling his neck. She stopped and retied it around him. Her left arm screamed with pain from using it, but she didn't have a choice. They had to get out of the house.

The crackling sound of the fire grew louder as though it were proclaiming it was coming to get them. The thought prodded her to move even faster.

Standing to the side, she struck the glass and it shattered. Knocking out the pieces that clung to the frame, she worked quickly, the stench of burning wood saturating the air. Then she went to the drawer where the towels and place mats were kept and grabbed an armful of them. After laying them along the bottom of the windowsill, she wheeled her father as close to the opening as she could.

His face pale, his eyes half-closed, he struggled to breathe. He was hacking so hard, he bent forward.

Smoke burned the back of her throat, stinging her eyes, but she ignored it. She had to get her father out.

Putting her good arm around him, she tried to lift him from the chair. He rose slightly, started coughing again and slumped back into her. She staggered, gasping for her own breath—each one full of smoke clawing its way down her throat. Threatening her.

The phone ringing sliced through the sounds of the fire growing closer.

Connor twisted the key in the ignition. Nothing happened. He tried again. Dead. His engine didn't even turn over. He pounded his palm into the steering wheel then thrust the door open.

Urgency spurred his pace. He charged back into the station, aware of each second slipping away.

"I need a car now. Mine is dead."

The deputy at the counter dug into his pocket and tossed him his keys. "The one closest to the sidewalk."

"Call the sheriff and let him know something is going down at Gramps's."

Connor whirled around and raced out of the office. Time was his enemy. His heartbeat outpaced his step as he moved to the cruiser and hoped it ran.

Cara wavered under the almost deadweight of her father. Every muscle trembled; her left arm refused to cooperate. Her cell phone rang in her pocket, but without letting her dad go, she couldn't get to it.

Help, Lord.

Securing her hold on her dad with her right arm only, she steeled herself and heaved him up. She managed to get him to his feet in front of the window. She bent him over and guided him through the opening. Smoke even drenched the air stirring outside.

"Dad, I'm pushing you through. Try to cushion yourself with your shoulders as you fall. I'll be right behind you." She stared at his face. His eyes red, he blinked several times.

As she laid him over the towels and mats, she glimpsed the distance to the ground. Four feet. *Please, Lord, protect him.*

Her dad helped some by throwing his weight forward, his body finally tumbling through the window. As soon as he disappeared through the opening, Cara followed suit, missing her father's prone body on the grass by a foot. Thankfully, she landed on her right side.

The wonderful sound of sirens—still several blocks away—competed with the noise of the fire. She looked toward the side of the house. Flames ate at the wood, especially around the base. Making its way toward them.

"Dad, we've got to get away from here." She crawled toward him to help him up.

The sight of his eyes closed scared her. She reached out to shake him. That was when her gaze turned to the bloodied rock by her father's head.

She found his pulse at his neck. *He's alive.* But he wasn't moving. Out cold.

Adrenaline and determination to keep them alive pumped energy into her exhausted body. Scrambling to her feet, using only her right arm, she began dragging him across the grass to safety.

A boom, like a piece of timber crashing down, quivered through the air. She peered toward the window where Mike's bedroom was. Once she got her father away from the house, she had to get Mike out, too.

But the fire continued to engulf the wooden structure, mocking her intent.

Her cell rang again. She fished for the phone, saw Connor's number and answered it. "The house is on fire. Your grandfather is still inside."

"I'm almost there. Right behind the fire trucks. Where are you?"

"I'm pulling Dad to safety in the backyard. He's passed out. Then I can go back in and…"

"No!" Connor's shout blasted her. Then in a softer voice he said, "I'll be there before you can do anything. Stay with your dad. Keep him safe."

"Okay." There was a part of her that wanted to protest what Connor asked her to do, but she knew he was right, especially as she focused on the burning house. The flames were attacking the second story now, the bottom one had surrendered to the inferno.

Slowly she hauled her father to a safe distance near the line of trees at the back of the fenced backyard. Her body aching, her throat burning like the house, she collapsed next to her father.

Sucking in gulps of air not as saturated with smoke, she listened as the fire trucks grew closer and closer.

With her eyes feeling like needles stabbed them, she closed them, coughs racking her with an intensity that doubled her over. Now that she was safe, it seemed like her body was shutting down—finally acknowledging what she'd been subjected to for the past ten minutes. Her coughs evolved into gasps as she drew in shallow breaths. Her lungs screamed for oxygen.

Maybe she could get to Mike before Connor? Logic told her both the back and front door were inaccessible. How would she get inside?

Still, she needed to try. She couldn't let him die.

She opened her eyes to the sound of movement to her left.

Black jeans-clad legs came into view. She fumbled for her gun at her waist as she scanned up the petite frame.

Her gaze collided with a weapon pointed at her.

Connor slammed on the brakes in front of Gramps's house, right behind the second fire truck. A second later, he raced across the grass toward the house on fire. Flames were shooting up toward the sky.

No, Gramps! The words roared through his mind like the sound of the fire roaring through the wooden structure of his childhood home.

From the side of the house, the state trooper staggered toward him. The guard held his head while he weaved as if he were avoiding some imaginary barriers.

Before Connor could, a firefighter made it to the officer and grabbed him, guiding him toward the street.

"What happened here?" Connor asked the state trooper

as they passed while his gaze swept the area for his grandfather.

"I don't know." The man swayed, his eyes dull, his speech slow. "I was hit—from behind."

Which meant the fire wasn't an accident—even though he hadn't thought it was—Connor had wished he'd been wrong. "Gramps? Have you seen him?" He spoke not only to the state trooper but to the firefighter.

"No," the officer mumbled then sank to the ground as his legs finally gave away.

Connor headed toward the house, scanning the top floor. The bottom was almost gone, and if his grandfather were alive, he would have to be up there—the east side where the damage wasn't as bad.

God, don't take him. Please.

He took his cell while he continued to search and placed a call to Cara to make sure she'd gotten far enough away from the house. It rang and rang and rang.

In the heat from the fire a chill encased Connor. She was in trouble. The person who had set this fire—Brandy?— had her or Cara would have answered the phone.

He pivoted toward the fire chief and shouted to him, "Gramps is still in the house."

"Connor," his grandfather's gravelly voice sounded above of the roar of the fire.

He glanced toward the right. His grandfather limped toward him with a firefighter helping him to walk, his legs wobbly.

"I've got to get to Cara."

Gramps nodded.

Connor jogged toward the side of the house, ignoring the shouts of the firefighters telling him to stay back. He skirted the burning structure as much as possible, but the scorch of the fire seared into him. The smoke invaded his lungs.

He didn't care. He had to reach Cara as fast as possible.

Looking down the barrel of a gun for the second time in a week, Cara went through a series of possible actions and came to the conclusion she was in the Lord's hands. She couldn't outrun a bullet.

Her assailant grinned, pure malice behind Brandy's— Sally's—expression. "Your dad won't get away this time."

She looked into the eyes of a killer and was glad her father was unconscious. He wouldn't know what happened to him. She glanced back at his prone body behind her and to her side.

Dad, I forgive you.

The sound of a gunshot blasted the air. Cara tensed.

Peering down at her chest, she saw blood on her white shirt, mingling with the dirt and grass smudges. Then she looked up.

Brandy stood, surprise wiping the grin from her face. Suddenly she crumbled to the ground. Behind her, Connor, with his gun drawn, rushed toward Cara.

Confusion, quickly followed by relief, flooded her. Her gaze riveted on the most beautiful sight—Connor.

He grabbed Brandy's gun, briefly checked her pulse, then continued to Cara. "She's alive." He stared at the red blotch on her shirt. "You're hurt."

She did, too. Her shoulder ached and was bleeding. "I reopened my wound. I'll be fine. It's Dad I'm worried about. He hit his head when he went out the window."

As the fire chief approached, Connor took out his cell and put a call in to Sean. Then the fire chief went to get help. People crowded the backyard as the blaze continued to destroy Mike's house.

Two days later, with her arm in a sling again, Cara stared at the calm waters of the lake, watching the sunrise peeping over the tops of the trees on the other side of the cove. The coolness in the early September morning air, streaked with yellows and oranges, lent a beauty to the dawn. It felt good to be alive. *Thank You, Lord.*

He was the reason she was standing on the shore, appreciating the start of a new day—a new life.

She needed to stay in Clear Branch for a while until her father was better. She'd realized that when she was protecting him. She could use the time to decide what she wanted to do with the rest of her life. Being a bodyguard had met a need for her once. Not anymore.

She caught a movement to the left of her and shifted around. Across the lawn of the lodge, Connor strode toward her, tired, several days' growth of beard on his face as if he had been up all night. Probably had. Before she'd gone to sleep in her room at the lodge, she'd talked with Mike, who was staying there, too. He mentioned Connor working around the clock to wrap up her father's case.

She remembered the scene in Mike's backyard thirty-six hours ago. Intense. Chaotic. She, Mike and her father were whisked to the hospital in Silver Springs. Thankfully, the fire chief had called an ambulance earlier. She and Mike had been released yesterday morning. Dad was still there to make sure he was stabilized, but he should be allowed to come home later today.

"Gramps told me you were out here." Connor gave her a smile, his eyes full of exhaustion.

"Have you gotten any sleep lately?"

"Not more than a catnap for the past forty-eight hours."

The weariness in his voice and face drew her closer to him. Before the fire he'd made it clear he needed to move on with his life. "Go get some sleep. You deserve it."

"I will, but I have one more thing I have to do."

"What?" She wanted to touch him, pull him close and wrap her arms about him, but the words they'd exchanged a few days ago stood in her way.

"This."

Connor stepped very close and hauled her into his embrace. His mouth descended on hers in a kiss that declared she was his. A kiss that healed her heart and soul. A kiss that gave her hope.

"I love you, Cara. Is there any way we can make this work between us? This past week I nearly lost you several times. When I saw Brandy pointing the gun at you, intending to kill you and your dad, I knew I couldn't lose you again for any reason. Life's too short not to grab love when it comes. What will it take to convince you we were meant to be together?"

"Mmm. Let me see. I could use another kiss."

He laughed and tightened his arms around her before accommodating her request.

Minutes later, he pressed her close to his side and strolled to a bench near the water. "I'm exhausted but I don't think I can sleep."

"Why not?" She snuggled against him.

"Too happy."

"We still have a lot to talk about."

"Yeah, I know," he said with a sigh.

"Is Dad safe from the gang?"

"When a deal was put on the table, good only for the first one to talk, Lucy got smart and told us what we needed to know. The other two will be charged to the full extent."

Brandy, who had set the fire and tried to kill her and her dad two days ago, was still in the hospital recovering from her gunshot wound. But she would live and would soon be transferred to a jail cell. "What kind of deal?"

"She's testifying against the other two and has cut a deal to give information concerning the two leaders in jail awaiting trial in exchange for going into the Witness Protection Program."

"What loyalty to her boyfriend."

"Which one, Beau or the lieutenant?"

"True," Cara said with a laugh. "Lucy is a woman who grabs the best opportunity for her, no matter who gets hurt in the process." She paused. "Why did they come after Dad in the first place? The story had already appeared in the news."

"Revenge, pure and simple. Brandy was the one who started the plot to kill your dad by making it look like John Smith had done it. She got Lucy to go along. Lucy told us she'd been afraid that if she didn't help they would think she wasn't one of them. My contacts told me Lucy had turned in Beau and started dating the lieutenant right before he was arrested. I think she was trying to prove herself to the gang since Beau had ratted on them."

"What about the gang member working with them? The one who came after you at the station?"

"Skull was the one who usually carried out the hits ordered by the leader. Lucy can give us names and dates of some of those hits."

Cara rested her head against Connor's shoulder, his minty scent drifting to her. "What about the other gang members? Couldn't they come after Dad?"

"Apparently when all this was going down this past month, there was a power struggle within the gang. It's under new leadership. The new head of the gang wants to distance himself from the former leaders. They are lying low. I understand they have made it clear no one is to harm you or your dad."

"Why did Skull come after you at the station?"

"I think he'd been following me and didn't want me to go to Gramps's before Brandy took care of you all." Connor hugged her and kissed the top of her head.

"I'm glad he didn't succeed stopping you. I wouldn't be here if he had."

"Me neither." A shudder passed down Connor's body. "I prefer not thinking about that consequence."

Cara pulled back and looked into Connor's eyes. "I called Kyra yesterday evening when I got back from visiting Dad at the hospital. I told her I was quitting. I'm staying here to take care of Dad until he gets back on his feet."

"What are you going to do after that?"

"That's a good question, but I have time to decide that." She cupped his face. "I do know one thing. I'm not leaving the state of Virginia anytime soon. I need to put down roots. I need something different than what I thought I wanted thirteen years ago. I'm not that same gal."

"As you're making plans for the future, I hope they include me because I want you in my life."

She leaned forward and brushed her lips across his. "You will figure prominently in my future. You're the man I love. Have always loved."

EPILOGUE

"Class, that's all for today. See you on Thursday." Cara snatched a hand towel from the back of the chair and wiped her face as her self-defense students filed out of the large studio in Richmond.

She spied her father weaving his way through the group of women leaving, still using a cane to walk a year and a half later. Other than that, he'd recovered quickly after his near death in the fire. The incident had given him the jolt he needed to dig in and work to regain his former skills. And to work to improve their relationship.

"What are you doing here? I thought you were going to be in Washington for a couple more days." Cara kissed his cheek then stepped back.

"Finished up early. Connor asked me to visit you two for a few days. He told me he'd meet me here so he could take us to dinner."

"So that's why he wanted me to bring a change of clothes here," Cara thought aloud.

"So, where is your husband?"

Cara scanned the studio. "He said he would be here right after my last self-defense class."

Her father grinned. "What's he up to?"

"He wanted to see you. It's been a month since we visited Clear Branch."

He shook his head. "We both know we aren't best friends. So give."

No, Connor and her dad weren't bosom buddies, but they did get along—mostly for her sake, and she appreciated not refereeing between them when they got together. And although she and her dad were finally forming a father-daughter relationship, it still had a ways to go. But after the fire, he'd changed in more ways than one—as though he'd been given a second chance and he'd decided not to mess it up.

She still didn't understand her parents' marriage, but once she forgave her father, it didn't matter. That was the past.

"Ah, here comes Connor."

Her husband strolled across the studio and gave her a kiss before greeting her dad. "Sorry I'm late. Traffic." Connor's gaze latched on to Cara's. "Why don't you go get changed and then we can go to dinner?"

"Hold it, you two. I'm not going anywhere until I know why I was asked to come to Richmond."

"Should I tell him or you?" Connor asked Cara.

"You orchestrated this. Be my guest."

"You're going to be a grandpa in about seven months."

Her dad didn't say anything for several long seconds, then the biggest grin spread across his face. "Now *that* is something to celebrate."

* * * * *

Dear Reader,

PROTECTING HER OWN is the second book in my Guardians, Inc., series about female bodyguards. I love writing about strong women who can take care of themselves in dangerous situations. For this story I had to put myself into the shoes of a man who had lost his ability to communicate well with others—a man whose job was in communications. I wanted to show the frustration and anger that occurs when someone loses a sense of who he is.

I love hearing from readers. You can contact me at margaretdaley@gmail.com or at P.O. Box 2074 Tulsa, OK 74101. You can also learn more about my books at: http://www.margaretdaley.com. I have a quarterly newsletter that you can sign up for on my website, or you can enter my monthly drawings by signing my guest book.

Best wishes,

Margaret Daley

QUESTIONS FOR DISCUSSION

1. The villain was motivated by revenge. How can we get past wanting to hurt someone we thought hurt us?

2. Cara began to doubt that the Lord cared about her. She'd prayed for help and didn't think she was getting any from Him. Have you ever thought that? What did you do?

3. Cara wondered why evil exists in the world. Have you ever wondered that? Why do you think evil exists?

4. Who is your favorite character? Why?

5. Cara and Connor were both exposed to a lot of evil in their job. They saw things that most people didn't. Connor believed what kept him going was his faith. Have you ever seen something horrific? How did you deal with the situation?

6. What is your favorite scene? Why?

7. Cara was burnt out and didn't know what she wanted to do professionally when she came to Clear Branch. Have you had a job that has left you burnt-out and floundering for a direction for your life? How did you get through it?

8. Connor was afraid to trust Cara with his heart again. Trust is important in a relationship. How do you establish trust with another?

9. Cara had a hard time accepting help from others. She'd learned in her job to work alone. Is it easy for you to accept help from people? If not, why do you have trouble with that? What are some ways people can get over thinking they have to do everything themselves?

10. Cara's relationship with her father was shaky. She blamed him for her mother's death. She had to learn to deal with her father in this story. What kind of relationship do you have with your father or mother? How can you make it better?

11. Cara's father suffered a stroke. He couldn't control much in his life. He even had a hard time expressing his thoughts to someone. This was difficult for a man who had always been so in control of his life. Have you been around someone who has had a stroke or a disease that has left that person depending on others? What are some things people can do to give the person dignity and a feeling of worth?

12. Cara felt guilty for causing a woman's death while she was protecting a client. In the process of protecting her client, another was shot. Cara didn't know how to work her way through her guilt. It was one of the reasons she had reached a crossroad in her life. How have you dealt with guilt?

13. Connor tried to help Cara with what was bothering her. Guilt can do a lot of harm to a person. How can guilt be displayed in someone? As a friend what can you do to help that person overcome his guilt?

14. Who do you think targeted Cara and her father? Why?

15. Cara needed to get her life on track. She needed to start over, doing something that would fulfill her. Have you ever done that? How did you start over? What helped you to do that?

16. Connor thought the best way he should deal with Cara at the start of the book was to keep his distance. She'd hurt him. He didn't want to get pulled into her life. Sometimes we can't avoid being around people who have hurt us. What are some things we can do to deal with people who have hurt us?

INSPIRATIONAL

Inspirational romances to warm your heart & soul.

Love Inspired
SUSPENSE

TITLES AVAILABLE NEXT MONTH
Available July 12, 2011

THE INNOCENT WITNESS
Protection Specialists
Terri Reed

HER GUARDIAN
Sharon Dunn

DEAD RECKONING
Rachelle McCalla

DANGEROUS REUNION
Sandra Robbins

LISCNM0611

REQUEST YOUR FREE BOOKS!

2 FREE RIVETING INSPIRATIONAL NOVELS
PLUS 2 FREE MYSTERY GIFTS

Love Inspired®
SUSPENSE

YES! Please send me 2 FREE Love Inspired® Suspense novels and my 2 FREE mystery gifts (gifts are worth about $10). After receiving them, if I don't wish to receive any more books, I can return the shipping statement marked "cancel". If I don't cancel, I will receive 4 brand-new novels every month and be billed just $4.24 per book in the U.S. or $4.74 per book in Canada. That's a saving of at least 23% off the cover price. It's quite a bargain! Shipping and handling is just 50¢ per book in the U.S. and 75¢ per book in Canada.* I understand that accepting the 2 free books and gifts places me under no obligation to buy anything. I can always return a shipment and cancel at any time. Even if I never buy another book, the two free books and gifts are mine to keep forever.

123/323 IDN FDCT

Name	(PLEASE PRINT)	
Address		Apt. #
City	State/Prov.	Zip/Postal Code

Signature (if under 18, a parent or guardian must sign)

Mail to the **Reader Service:**
IN U.S.A.: P.O. Box 1867, Buffalo, NY 14240-1867
IN CANADA: P.O. Box 609, Fort Erie, Ontario L2A 5X3

Not valid for current subscribers to Love Inspired Suspense books.

**Are you a subscriber to Love Inspired Suspense
and want to receive the larger-print edition?
Call 1-800-873-8635 or visit www.ReaderService.com.**

* Terms and prices subject to change without notice. Prices do not include applicable taxes. Sales tax applicable in N.Y. Canadian residents will be charged applicable taxes. Offer not valid in Quebec. This offer is limited to one order per household. All orders subject to credit approval. Credit or debit balances in a customer's account(s) may be offset by any other outstanding balance owed by or to the customer. Please allow 4 to 6 weeks for delivery. Offer available while quantities last.

Your Privacy—The Reader Service is committed to protecting your privacy. Our Privacy Policy is available online at www.ReaderService.com or upon request from the Reader Service.

We make a portion of our mailing list available to reputable third parties that offer products we believe may interest you. If you prefer that we not exchange your name with third parties, or if you wish to clarify or modify your communication preferences, please visit us at www.ReaderService.com/consumerschoice or write to us at Reader Service Preference Service, P.O. Box 9062, Buffalo, NY 14269. Include your complete name and address.

Read on for a preview of the first book in the heartwarming new ROCKY MOUNTAIN HEIRS *series,* THE NANNY'S HOMECOMING *by Linda Goodnight, on sale in July from Love Inspired.*

Gabe Wesson was a desperate man.

Inside the Cowboy Café, a hodgepodge of various other townsfolk gathered at the counter for homemade pie and socializing. Gabe sat on a stool, his toddler son, A.J., on his knee.

He'd discovered that if a man wanted to know anything in the town of Clayton, Colorado, the Cowboy Café was the place. Today, what he needed more than anything was a nanny.

He'd found Clayton, a sleepy community time had forgotten. With an abandoned railroad track slicing through town and an equally abandoned silver mine perched in the nearby hills, the town was just about dead.

It was the just-about that had brought Gabe to town. He had a knack for sniffing out near-dead businesses and resurrecting them.

But unless he found a nanny for A.J. soon, he would be forced to move back to Denver.

On the stool next to Gabe, a cowboy-type angled a fork toward the street. A white hearse crept past. "They're planting old George today."

"Cody Jameson, show some respect," red-haired Erin Fields, the surprisingly young café owner, said. "This town wouldn't exist without George Clayton and his family. Speaking ill of the dead doesn't seem right. His grandkids are here for the funeral and *they're* good people. Brooke Clayton came in yesterday. That girl is still sweet as that cherry pie."

Gabe listened with interest, gleaning the facts and the undercurrents. He wondered if George's heirs knew he'd sold the mine to an outsider.

Gabe and A.J. stood and pushed out into the summer sun as the last of the funeral cars crawled by. A pretty woman with wavy blond hair gazed bleakly through the passenger window. Something in her expression touched a chord in him. He knew he was staring but couldn't seem to help himself. The woman looked up. Their eyes met and held. Sensation prickled Gabe's skin.

The car rolled on past and she was gone. But the vision of Brooke Clayton's sad blue eyes stayed behind.

George Clayton's will stipulates that his six grandchildren must move back to their tiny hometown for a year in order to gain their inheritance. With her life in shambles, Brooke Clayton is the first to comply. Could she be the answer to Gabe's prayers?

Look for THE NANNY'S HOMECOMING
by Linda Goodnight available in July
wherever books are sold.

SHLIEXP0711

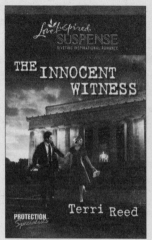